D0982493

Fiction

The Sky Changes
Steelwork
Imaginative Qualities of Actual Things
Splendide-Hôtel
Flawless Play Restored: The Masque of Fungo
Mulligan Stew
Aberration of Starlight
Crystal Vision
Blue Pastoral
Odd Number
A Beehive Arranged on Humane Principles

Poetry

The Darkness Surrounds Us
Black and White
The Perfect Fiction
Corrosive Sublimate
A Dozen Oranges
Sulpiciae Elegidia: Elegiacs of Sulpicia
White Sail
The Orangery
Selected Poems 1958-1980

Criticism

Something Said

Rose Theatre

Rose Theatre

Gilbert Sorrentino

The Dalkey Archive Press

Portions of this work have appeared in *Conjunctions, PsychCritique,* and *The Review of Contemporary Fiction,* to whose editors the author gives grateful acknowledgment.

ISBN: 0-916583-23-6
Library of Congress Catalog Card Number: 87-071643

Partially funded by grants from The National Endowment for the Arts and The Illinois Arts Council

The Dalkey Archive Press
1817 79th Avenue
Elmwood Park, IL 60635 USA

Who cares what was there before? There is no going back,
For standing still is death, and life is moving on,
Moving on towards death. But sometimes standing still is also life.

—*John Ashbery*

Chayne of dragons

Baal, the cat, King of the Invisible. In France, the girl on a rock in a field, thighs pressed modestly together. Off-white raw silk shift, a peach-colored silk slip with white lace hem and bodice. A full bottle of Bromo-Seltzer. "What a Girl!" Go *slow*. It is Bune, the Dragon of the Dead, who terrifies the filthy streets. That eerie café in Ferozepore, the Punjab? Dog walker! She is dusting. Like the libidinous Charlotte Bayless, she wants a lengthy sojourn in the Bahamas, preferably with Lou Henry, the humiliated goat. Agares, Master of Tongues and Crocodiles, vacationing in Fanapa. He speaks sweetly, sweetly to three young girls on a brilliant green lawn, one in a summer dress, the other two in pullovers and short pants or are they in black evening gowns of some shiny metallic fabric and peach-colored silk slips with white lace hems and plain bodices? The Tarot of Arthur Edward Waite: "He's a Voyeur." Go *fast* for Ronobe, Master of Rhetoric. And then be still as death. Flint, City of Promise? Sales correspondents all! She is sweeping. The lewd Flo Dowell, on a weekend in Paris with Guy Lewis, demon of drunkenness. Vassago, by whom the hidden is revealed, displays, from Antoine's seamy past, four smiling young women, four smiling young men, all in white: a rustic picnic table: tall drinks raised in a toast to grey tweed skirts, peach-colored silk slips with plain hems and white lace bodices. A paperback copy of *La musique et les mauvaises herbes.* "Jacks or Better." Go easy, whispers Berith, the Red Soldier of the Lie. Dost fornicate in wild abandon, thou base prevaricator? *Vide* the charming West Village that recalls the glory years of Lady Day. Pander! She is polishing. Filthy Yvonne Firmin, a month in the mountains visible in her dreams, close in the arms of Leo Kaufman, leveler of lays, ravager of rhymes. Gamygyn, who bears messages from dead sinners to Fantoine, to the vast and ornate dining room of the Splendide-Lincoln, on whose tables are strewn grey tweed jackets and peach-colored silk slips with plain hems and bodices. A half-empty package of Camels. "A Laff a Minute!" *Harder!* for the delectation of Astaroth, Angel of Unearthly Beauty, who hides his face in gorgeous masks of absolute corruption. Does he miss Clappeville, desolate amid the Alps? Croupier! She is vacuuming, naked, lascivious Emma Woodhouse, whose day at the beach was often spent beneath the panting Dick Detective, whining for his wife. Marbas, the Transformer, who lifts his wand before Agapa, changing himself to a ten-year-old boy in a striped polo shirt squinting at the sun, filled with blistering thoughts of rayon scarves and peach-colored lace hems with plain bodices, no slips. An empty leather tobacco pouch redolent of rum, maple, chocolate. "Two Guys from Hackensack." Deeper! Forneus, the Evil from the Sea, bellows, rising dripping, lusting for a tall, an icy Trommer's in Hackettstown, where Modernism died. Con artist, she is cooking, the horny Nora Avenel, anticipating a trip up the Hudson on the day line with Bart Kahane, maker of false idylls. Valefor, Mentor of Thieves, secluded in an English garden with Sir Bloom and Lord Bury playing patient and doctor, one in a pale blue silk tailored blouse, the other in a peach-colored lace bodice, plain hem, no slip. A beautiful doll dressed as a nurse. "On Their Metal." *Now!* Foras, Great President of Strength, looks on: to whom all the world doth kneel. In Malibu, whose sands are hot and blue, a game-show host! She is scrubbing. Dirty Lydia Languish, on a picnic in the woods, accidentally strips before the eyes of Anton Harley, the razer of kitchens. Amon, who vomits fire on seeing Sylvie Lacruseille, or is it Ann Taylor Redding, sunbathing on a Manhattan rooftop in an ounce of spandex. By her bronzing side a pair of smoke-shade nylon stockings, a colored lace bodice, no peaches. A forged Fragonard. "Cartel." I'm *going* to. Asmoday, Familiar of the Cur from Hell, yet clothed impeccably in natural fabrics, dreams of the Cotswolds where the sheep run for their very lives. Preacher, she is washing! Ruttish Zuleika Dobson on a Sunday in Central Park ogles Biff Page, whose eyes are amethyst and neon. Barbatos, who understands the birds, in a metallic room filled with photographs of Sheila Henry at ten, smiling from the back seat of her father's Packard outside Nathan's Famous in Coney Island. He is buying beige nylon stockings, colored lace peaches, but neither bodices nor hems. An alto saxophone reed once used by *Jimmy Dorsey?* "Old

Hoboken." Are you going to, too? Gaap, who makes insensible, now reigns, Master of Earthquakes, Reciter of Verse. That was in Callipolis, where Love Triumphed. Registered nurse! She is drying. She is sluttish Grace Armstrong, soon to take a stroll through Chinatown for an assignation with Harlan Pungoe, ruiner of souls. Paimon, obedient to Him who was drowned in the depths of His knowledge, beguiled by a steel evening gown; or the perfect image of a perfect navel orange on which has been neatly lettered in black ink, Ceci n'est pas une orange; or black silk full-fashioned stockings and a peaches and cream lace slip with no bodice. A copperplated ear trumpet bought in a Bleecker Street "sundries shop." "What's for Supper?" Ohhhh. Furfur, Earl of Married Love, who haunts the shadowed pools dark in the Poconos, Scranton of the Seven Caesars. High-powered executrix (she irons). Simmering Esther Summerson, off for a week in those fastnesses, fleeing from Barry Gatto, the underground duke. Buer, the Healer, seduced by Corrie and Berthe via an old photograph album whose every caption reads "Some Fun." In white nylon panties with white lace trim and a peaches and bodice hem and no slip, why not? A Tom Mix telescope carelessly displayed. "Blind Bums." Uhhh. Solas, Bleak Raven of Astronomy, who flies in candlelight forever more. Or to Natchitoches, redolent of chicory and jumpy jass. Building contractor. She is mending? Hot Betty Barker, fresh from a few days in Mazatlán where Rupie sucked on her pumps. Gusion, the Duke of Those Who Discern, with disembodied voice that speaks of Durga, Goddess of Destruction, the clumsy brass figurine of Whom has its nipples rendered prominent by two dabs of nail polish, Red Moon. She hath scorned the black lace corselette with bodice of lace cream and peach hem. A key, to a suite, in the Blue Runes, motel. "The Heart is Lo-onely." Ooohhh. Marchosias, the Wolf, hideth his phiz amid a crowd of galaxies. Above Charleville? Where poor Arthur saw the Northern Lights? Demolition expert, "she" is sewing. Lustful May Fielding on a hike in the woods so wild espied Henri Kink, the living corpse, amid various items of decay. Sytry, jussus secreta libenter detegit feminarum; or, a ventriloquist's dummy; or, a doll dressed as Sister Philomena Veronica, whose black stiletto heels shine beneath the hem of her chaste habit, peachy. White cotton p-----s and more white cotton "things." A discarded typescript of a Ph.D. dissertation on Lorenzo's lost novel, *Marmalade Eros.*

"World of Signs." Oh *God!* Phoenix, who lispeth as a child, hunts amid the hollyhocks for "Sis," dreams of Mytilene, a snatch of honey, φαίνεταί μοι, humble bard, she is knitting. Steamy Donna Julia, after an hour in the pool, caresses Sol Blanc, the sun twin, excites Antony Lamont the other secluded in the Plaza with nymphomaniacal Venetia Herbert she fucks the languorous police chief eyes "cast" toward Staten Island rich world of Gotham content at last in her middle years but for Furcas the Cruel Elder open wide A Batch of Stuff including pale blue file folders and a Ship 'n' Shore flowered print blouse white Mary Janes at this Cecil Tyrell predictably scowls at the "blank" sheet of paper predictably rolled into his predictable Royal Manual studied clutter Glasyalabolas the Murderer of Barnett Tete of owning of hoarding of purveying dear and yet a fiesta in Old Méjico discovers him paying voluptuous Katie Woodward for unspeakable favors she tidies dressed as a "French" "maid" like Binghamton like on the mother-fucking road sport all trapped in their own circumferential evidence as Procel the Geometer has so proven put it in! Win a Bundle or a treatise on fractals or Habits and Wimples and bone Mary Janes *plus* a passport-size photograph of Henri Kink face twisted with terror albeit well-groomed as per Naberius the Cock of Cocks Duke Washington of heresy of blasphemy of cant of Labor Day weekend in Madrid with depraved Eleanor Harding who arranges for the bartender in Aspen a last resort Yours For No Down Payment Easy Terms Hagenti Maker of Gold do you like *that* Regular Guy? beside a Hudson Terraplane in orange silk dress and tan "things" then *see* "Scale model of Splendide-Malibu in the lobby of Splendide-New Haven" attractive yet stern Aini the Destroyer Chico of the flickering image e. g. a holiday in Sun Valley e. g. the whorish Amelia Sedley she stores (stares) so says the maitre d' in the inn at Sciacca the "roots of confidence" at the "Snorter" neo-impressionist minimalist star with bankable first novel screenplay inside Vual Camel of Egypt I *like* that La Última Despedida but to a pair of *drumsticks?* to a pair of glasses with tortoiseshell frames and brown shoesies to a photograph of three young couples the women disconcertingly identical outside London laughs Ipos the Angelic Lion as Biggs Richard of anonymous January in Monte Carlo New Jersey in pursuit of lecherous Nancy Lammeter she mops she is a chef in Frisco city of cupcakes where ensues the search for the perfect pome and

where lives Bifrons Disturber of the Dead *more!* Guy Ropes! in the
sunshaft a fly in amber a tortoiseshell barrette a pair of some goddamned things in the gloaming old Rupe again avidly staring at some
bulging oranges the "real thing" but the wall collapses before the
assault of Morax the Bull *cum* Cecil the cursed the blasted a fortnight in
a Kenya of the imagination ah the debauched Alice Bridgenorth she
cleans a "food server" lost in Cortland where the virtuoso singer died
dancing in the haunted wood of carrion memory Vine Monster of
Witches *don't! stop!* Every Girl's Dream a copy of the Irish folktale
bedad begorrah bejayzus *The Paddy in the Brake* soon to be a pair of
stack-heeled shoes with small silver buckles isolate a self-portrait of
René Magritte contemplating a photograph of a photograph of a
painting of a perfect navel orange paired with Durga and Purson of
Bears of Trumpets of Jackson Towne duke of the sticks on the town in
town and in shameless dalliance with the wanton Dorothea Brooke who
prunes and how a college traveler who goes broke in Brooklyn limbo of
small griefs a vague backdrop of uncertain smiles Shax Destroyer of the
Understanding stop! Ladders at Last and a matchbook from Helen and
Troy's café within whose ladies' room a pair of black steel pumps on
whose heels is impaled the first card The Magician of the Greater
Arcana large calves and slender ankles whispers Saleos the Pander and
so Page Moses the doctor of plots writes of a "trip" to the "moon" and
the immodest Lucy Brandon his heroine she plants she is a shipping
clerk in Colma city of crypts and cadavers while rain lashes the
windows Vepar Duke of Storms and Tempests like *that!* You're the
Top you're a box of cookies you're a single red sling high-heeled shoe in
the hand of a young man in electric-blue suit whose lapel button's
printed message is too small to read? "small silver buckles"? Bathin of
the Pale Horse Lincoln Gom falsifier of artisans a Saturday in
Monterey the unchaste Edith Granger weeds candy maker of Jersey
City of bitter Februaries of despair in driving sleet bad Chinese food
Sabnack Marquis of Wounds and Worms hath himself prepared like
this? Thinking of You a full set of steel false teeth in one cup of a white
nylon brassiere et au milieu d'un essaim de filles Madame Lorpailleur
nue tirait la langue tirait les white silk pumps by Botis the Viper Vance
Whitestone he who rapes a year in Calafawnya as the impure Letitia
Snap she waters the bell-ringer? thence to Manhattan a fifth of old Noo

Yawk eater of pies kneader of dough Focalor Drowner of Men sweetheart! An Idiot's Pleasure a blackjack a white lace brassiere sweat-
stained somebody's dear old mother in the act of placing a pie on a
windowsill stern but comely Zepar who drives women mad with lust
thus Horace Rosette the collector one time in Gstaad appalled by the
indecent Tabitha Bramble she gardens a perfect hostess he thought of
Hartford where a fat man lusted for his "lineage" in another life a
certain Mr. Anthony no names pliz or Raum He Who Reconciles?
baby! Chattering Fools some decayed costumes e.g. white nylon garter
belts with lace front panels (nota bene a strange incomprehensible
construction in metal) tortoiseshell peaches the delight of Eligor the
Lustful the Concupiscent the Seductive John Hicks killer of the aged
hidden in the night in Tunisia wild with the fantasies of salacious
Margaret Ramsay she airs but a dishwasher years ago in Haddam Neck
of the right graveyards the right house with large loft with kiln therein
with books scattered "about" Malpas Friend of False Artificers Christ!
Lengthy and Serious Talks bits of dark silk white lace French something a still of Tania Crosse in vile embrace with two popular female
stars of rival network news "shows" short-haired Lerajie Creator of
Strife all will be metamorphosed forever by Beleth the Terrible and
Halpas Burner of Cities the fearsomely regal and beautiful the black
heifers of chaos those who persuaded the joyous Irishman to don a
scanty daringly short skirt riding up at the knee to show a peep of white
pantalette transparent stockings emeraldgartered with the long straight
seam trailing up beyond the knee who placed *The Secrets of the Bottom
Drawer* under his oxter who created Yonkers by which some came by
way of who filled with malice invented the pink jersey sleeveless dress
for hapless women the sculpture *The Caliph Lorzu* fashioned by them
and into the mouths of lovers they have placed the words "no bananas"
have defiled obscenely the obscene Esther Waters who spit on Jesus
darkness falls at their behest on any day on all days and Saul Blanche at
their pleasure is become the Sun Twin. AND at their command enters
Baal: who hath transformed his image to that of the slavering brach:
who hath become visible.

Littel alter

Introibo ad altare Dei . . . many ascents, but always laid low. She went forth to battle but she always fell. Usually on her back. Laid is good. You couldn't count them all if you tried. The T-shirt, the paisley tie, the old khakis, the seersucker suit. Chicks really dig it. The paisley tie came all over himself, the old khakis had a wife and children. The seersucker suit quoted Anatole Broyard. The T-shirt, which T-shirt? That one, that one, that one, that one, that one. You're the top, you're a gonococcus. And this one is Jimmy, in the wading pool, he's four, and Marge has on the Hofstra sweatshirt, she just turned seven. Is she cute or is she cute? Spurted all over himself, the poor man. Dick knew but did Dick care? Dick was an ascots. Dick was a desert boots. Dick was a faded blue chambray shirts. Bach. If there's anything she could *not* stand! Jesus Christ Almighty and His Blessed Mother. I can't get away to marry you today, Karen. Whore of the airways. How about this, baby? She thought she invented it. Did you ever see anything like this, honey? Hell, half the world has one. My wife won't let me. Let him what? The photographer will snap *her,* God knows. God damn him and his boils and his impeccable handkerchief. He was kneeling, well-trained Catholic that he is, or was. *He* was kneeling too, his Nikon or his Kodak or whatever. She'll never tell. She never told. Who would have thought that poetical Dick would grieve in his lust? Because of some pictures? Well, men. Often, when she knelt to kiss the crucifix, she knew that rubbers and frayed collar was looking at her. From there it was but a step to T-shirt and seersucker suit, not to mention old khakis and all those impossible snapshots. If that stairwell could talk. It would say *Kyrie eleison.* God sees all from the altar and it is a sin to laugh in his house. It's also a sin to show your underpants. Once a bad girl, always. Dick, thtay? Caw and thay you have to meet thomebody? My wife won't let me. There she was, waiting at the church. Have a

13

Manhattan? Tastes like horse piss, hahaha. Uncle Johnny was a real card. Is that the Lido I see? Do Not Disturb. Or only Asbury Park? Do Not Disterb. The dumb bastards. He said he spread all my pictures out on the bed and did it. He loved her with his boils and all. His imported beer and his cheddar and his English Ovals and his Bach and his amethyst crystal ashtrays. Do not disturb! Do you see this brand-new drawing? Got it just the other day. The French bitch with the Gitanes. Smoke that cigarette, Annie so-called, so-called Annie, Gitanes for her, her for Gitanes. Eez zat ow you say? Zat eez ow we say, ow do you say in ze Yonkers? His wife won't let him. Is it possible that on her wedding day she actually wore a girdle? Uncle Johnny and his rented royal blue tux, Knights of Columbus, Confraternity of the Most Precious Blood, and although her body was her most sacred temple and altar. Oh Johnny. Did Dick care? Mr. Boils, meet Mr. Pimples. Care for a double-thick chocolate shake and a large fries? It was great Art what rescued him from his bourgeois sleep. Bach definitely smoked English Ovals and sat in a rocking chair. To listen to his own records. His wife won't let him but did he give a goddamn? Karen Gash put the steak on and love sweet love just like in the movies. Down on his knees before *her* altar. Oh Johnny. The Manhattans taste like you'll pardon my French horse piss haha but what the hell, it's not every day your favorite niece contracts to get her ashes hauled. Do Not Disterb. It was the McCoy, a honeymoon suite from which the ocean could be glimpsed. In the dark, in Asbury Park, for a lark. Quark quark. *Finnegans Wake* that's from. Art which rescued him from the provincial. Right. Quark you. Oh Dick, the thteak is wuined. Just like in the movies. With ascot all undone and in a generally unbuttoned state, the young woman but partially dressed, he ascendeth to the Seventh Heaven. A far cry from Mechanicville. A girdle! That was in another country, you can bet the rent on that. He preferred *Dubliners,* yes, I prefer *Dubliners,* to tell the truth. Self-denigrating smile. To tell the what? Father Graham turned to face them, his best vatic smile beaming. It's a sin to laugh in church. It's a sin to tell a lie. What was that snowman story? If his nose were a carrot he'd eat it? Something about a roaring blaze in the old stone fireplace that makes her sick to her stomach. Gathered about the cheerful hearth, warm false friends all. What in the hell did she know about gardening that she should be on her knees in the mud? It's a treat to beat your feet. His meat. That's nice, oh that's good. Bless me Father, for I have sinned. It's been a hundred years since my last confession. I ate meat on Friday. What kind? She knew what Horace was going to show her that night. They all went crazy then. From pimples and boils to novel in progress. By the time she knew what had hit him, oh, the hell with it. She doethn't wike youw witing at aw, Dick? Not at all, face turned toward the window, the stricken artist. Now suck me off, O.K.? Mr. Suave. Off they went into the blue of the sky, *another* Karen. Every time she turns around he's humping *some* Karen. Norwegian beauty. Have another slab of lute-fiske? How about a passel of fried lingonberries? Or would you prefer some hot Scandinavian tongue? You must avoid the occasions of sin, my dear. She walked toward the altar, the faces of her old boring friends around her, the dusty rose coat, the lavender suit, the fuchsia hat, with veil. Beneath the finery, what else? Girdles. How do you like the opening sentence of chapter three? Through the humid indigo pall that had dropped on the island came pallid, distant voices, seemingly oblivious to the heat, lost, far, drowning in ecstacy. His desert boots. Throw another log on the fire, let's have a drink, put some Bach on, let's smoke a little dope, let's build a *snowman.* If his ear were a cunt, is that how it goes? The only surprise was that Dick was not another ascendant star in Harlan's galaxy. Speak nothing but good of the crippled. And the dead. Did she mention the cardboard living? Dick was probably with Tania, plenty of times. I don't think it's demeaning or anti-feminist for a woman to wear, well, exciting lingerie. Not at all, as a matter of fact, I think that. A woman. Is even. More. Womanly. On the weekends she can put on a Good Will fedora and a pair of overalls. Let's haul out the old stump afore we plow the bottom forty and save another miserable whale. Nota bene: black lace crotchless panties. Just the thing for those impromptu protest rallies. Fads and fancies. Speaking of such, the guy with the *shoes.* Some kind of gofer for Annette with the metal walls and the weird voice. That guy who wanted to marry Tania told me that there was some kind of an altar. How about collecting, you know, nothing spectacular, but like books? To screw Cecil, for one, is a boon to all mankind, Christ knows. He'll *never* die. Lou said it was an accident, sure, like Uncle Johnny's hand under my dress. Sorry to lose my favorite niece, now just let me get my hand in there. Just drunk, Dick said, hell, he's just a pathetic old drunk. Then she found two pairs of her panties missing, well, better them than me. Goils, duh blood streaming down Ah Lady's face from huh eyes, streaming down dat poifect, holy face, is blood shed because of duh sins of impurity occasioned by duh organs of sight, *ah* eyes. Ah Lady's heart is broken because of duh impure books and magazines and fillums dat tempt you on every side. Our Lady should have been at Horace's that night. Rose as the nun in what was it? *Sisters of Shame?* Underneath her habit a black corset, lace garters. God protect me, the priest said, as he pulled his pants off to reveal. Another Academy Award performance from Chet somebody. Bart finally went crazy, won't you sample some of this scent? Ce Soir. She sacrificed her whole youth for him. For what? What did she get? Older she got. She got I think I love Karen. Which one? Another one. She really knows how to haul your codfish, right, you louse? She actually prayed that his boils would come back and by Jesus they did. *Deo gratias.*

Lavabo inter innocentes manus meas . . . cross-eyed Maureen Shea caught her bouquet, so dumb she thought men had perpetual erections. Would it be any different if they did? And was she any the worse off? Than the rest? Of us? All of the lavender suits? If he hadn't met that jerk Leo he'd still be drinking beer in his T-shirt and playing the pinball machine out at Lena's Rest. I've been reading these fabulous poems baby, listen, what if a much of a wind of which. Jerry Casey figured that he'd turned into a fruit. Dear God, the ignorance of the thickhead. Dick knew. Dick was a T-shirts. Dick was an engineer's boots. Dick was a sideburns. Then Dick was a little treasury of modern poetry. When something punishes my hair with frozen fingers we'll love each other or die. The first time she went down on him, in the back seat of Billy Magrino's Dodge. And have you committed any sins of impurity, my child? I ate meat on Friday, Father. Chet somebody pulled his priestly pants off. To reveal to Sister Rose. What a bunch. I'm breaking off with her, I swear, I swear it, I am, so Dick said after they bumped into her with another Miss Shredded Wheat in Gimbels. Uh, this is, uh, this is, uh, uh, this is my, uh, wife, April. Innocent act, the two Misses Shredded Wheat with the blank skies of Iowa in their perfect faces. Did she deserve this humiliation? After she did what she did and never mind what, she washed her hands for fifteen minutes. A living cliché, that's what I am. Cross-eyed Maureen told Dolores who told Liz who told Georgene who told Terry who told Charlotte and Virginia who told Mary who told Nancy who told Nina what she did. I thought you were supposed to be my friends. I'm a whore, all *right.* Then, by Christ, let's do it! Bless me Father, for I have sinned, but I have washed my hands a lot. Yes, more than one. A man's got to have steady nookie, that's what he said, nookie, or else his brain will be affected. Must mean that none of you are getting laid. Good old Leo. Wike thith, Dick, baby? I love my wife. He loves the girl he's near, *pace* Ellen. Say girl to her and her fedora explodes. Her overalls melt. Her jockey shorts burst into flame. I want you to get my April home by twelve-thirty, Dick. Yes, I sure will, I'll just have to see to it that I pop her by midnight. By the light of the silv'ry moon. I washed with toilet paper in the stall at the Round Lake Inn, dancing every weekend to Mel Proud and His Melodics. Let's face the music. Kid. Do you want to come in? Is your mother still up? I think so. No. Why don't we do it right here on the porch? Is that you, dear? Jesus fucking Christ! She entered, her innocent smile conveying to all there gathered around the cheerful hearth the warmth and quiet benevolence of her mind and the purity and calm of her womanly heart. Eyes cast down, she blushed at praise of her goodness, protesting that she did not deserve such, in that they, in the humble performance of a steadfast charity, were more worthy of *her* encomia. In the modest reticule clasped firmly by her pale and delicate hand, her undergarments were discreetly hidden from their view, lest knowledge that she was naked beneath her dress should cause them to suspect her ruin. Didn't Dick want to come in? No, Mom, it's late, and besides, Dick is out in the wind and rain, behind yon stately elm, whacking himself off, I have little doubt. What a nice boy! So considerate. Yet won't he go crazy as well as impair his health? Hello! Hello, Maureen. How's Dick? Oh, we're separated, I'm afraid. Really? Yes, he said he needed his freedom in order to bring his notebook up to date. Really? Yes. His notebook? Yes. Well, I've got to run. Nice seeing you, cockeyes, keep your legs closed. She has eleven children by now, a little late. Well, he might as well be keeping his notebook up to date, the damn fool. They were all invited to a snow party at our house on January 14, 15, 16, they were to bring warm clothes and big appetites, there were to be cocktails and a snow-ball fight and cocktails. Please come! RSVP. If she ever *hears* the name

Robinson Jeffers again! The really interesting aspect is the unique, the savage imagery, really, an absolute genius. Among these learned innocents, no respite. And here's the fat guy who lives with his mother. And here's the maiden that men forget. And here's the girl who used to swing down on the garden gate. Yes, he'd sooner kill a man than a hawk. What a guy! Right, like Himmler. Somebody lost his jockey shorts. What *was* that snowman story? If his ear were a cock? The crackling blaze and Ted the bore going on and on about how Kline this and Rothko that and Motherwell's problem. She left to take a bath and was not seen among the revelers for twenty-four hours. You are some bitch treating my friends like that! Right. If I were an ear, would you fuck me? Karen, the twat of the clouds, smiled that smile what melts all manly hearts. Oh get the hell out of here with your idiot whore! Everything but true love. She could almost hear his back breaking out in boils. Go and wash yourself, you insulting bastard, I can *smell* the whore off you. *Lavabo inter innocentes,* thus spake Father Richard, S.J., crestfallen at this unfounded accusation. Cutesy Karen Wyoming, pulling on her cutesy bootsies, ith it thtill thnowing, Dick? And Bach labored on. Yes, baby, it is. I hope we can get to the aiwport on timey-wimey, my wove. If he's going to with Sheila she's going to with Lou. What a sap, yet those innocent tears after the accident or whatever were real. But that other guy in the car she wouldn't trust as far as she could throw him. They say he told everything they asked him. Just off the funny farm. He burned down some hotel or something. Cleanse me of my sins, shrive me of my few transgressions, I didn't know what I was doing. Fuck off, whoever you are. Dick was doing it with Sheila? I was doing it with Lou! Not a bad man except for his taste in what? Wives. Cold love, blue love, everything but true. True love breaks out in boils and pimples while he whacks off on his knees, weeping, forgive me, forgive me, oh, forgive me! She remembered his panegyric on the sound of the surf, did she not? Sheer poesy, Dick, just sheer, sheer voibal art. You are a bitch, a grade-A *bitch.* The crackling fire. The cheerful hearth. Good food and drink, ho! And the marvelous snowman, he melted. To treat my *friends* like this! Oh go write another dumb sentence you dumb, dumb, you dumb. And so, by God, he would. There is no stopping the obsessed artist. He'll show her that he's not just another sweaty schmuck beyond yon stately elm! It is with this, his first novel, that Richard Detective, whom most of us had secretly deemed an idiot, has produced the sort of work that helps keep us *all* in business. Indeed, transcending the finely etched chiaroscuro of inner truth and the inner depth of naturally rendered detail we feel that we have come to know as well as share in some inner beauty that is something and also something else. As she read, eyes cast down upon the crisp *Times,* she blushed. Where do they get these jerks? The structure of the novel is wholly satisfying, although, and yet, and yet, although. Finally, we come to appreciate the fine eye for this and the excellent ear for that. Where? From the far reaches of glittering Manahatta, yet few can find their way to Baltic Street or Tremont Avenue. Does it matter? Without them how could one dis-cover what one must know in order to understand? What? Shop on, shop on! Pre-washed, pre-torn, pre-faded and presented for your delectation along with a brief telephone interview, wholly illuminating. Often, Bach hovered in the background. Dick was the sort of man who washed his hands before listening to that fucking organ. So *much* Bach, yet where was he to turn for succor? Well, Karen Blonde and Karen Teeth were really nice and understood things. Also liked it in every orifice, right, hubby mine? So, taken all in all, we can take it all in all. Out to the parking lot, Vince Esposito smiled, climbing into his car. So long. I think, he thinks, I think I've fallen in love with Karen Com-plexion. Because of the sins of impurity occasioned by my eyes perusing *Baron Darke of Eagle House,* who, with insistent hands tore open Melissa's bodice so that her innocent breasts were exposed to his devouring gaze, the blood streamed from Our Lady's eyes down her sad and suffering face, for she abused herself with a bottle of Prell shampoo. When you abuse yourself with a bottle of Prell shampoo or anything else, Our Lady has a hemorrhage, right there on the little side altar. Absolutely. The guy, what was his name, said that the room was *freezing.* And with an altar. Such goings on were called fads and fancies. How about this, baby? I think it's much better. Through the oppressive wet indigo of the island night came distant pallid cries, lost in the maddening heat, ecstatic, perverse. The idiot, oh, the goddamned idiot. You were always a cheap philandering louse, long, long before Karen Cornfield. What? Why? Why? You don't remember that even when we were engaged you couldn't keep your eyes off dusty rose coat and lavender suit and fuchsia hat, with veil? All my boring friends, their

mouths working over the body and blood, dreaming of for Christ sake
Tab Hunter pulling their girdles off? Young people must, uh, avoid
these occasions of sin, girls, uh, no less than boys. Abjure that, uh, lewd
bottle of Prell! Discard that concupiscent, uh, candle! Jettison, oh
jettison that, uh, suggestive cucumber! In other woids, boin. Or marry
that nice, well, that O.K. boy with the station wagon has a good job in
insurance. She *knew* what Horace was going to show her. Warm
phonies all gathered about the old stone hearth of the house built in the
seventeen hundreds, the wraiths of Christ knows how many Protestants
about. Do you want to know what I think about Robinson Jeffers? He's
a prick. Jesus, if only all you drunks would tell the truth, just once. I'm
going to take a bath. That's *enough,* April. Enough my ass, nothing is
enough with you! His best vatic smile, it beamed. Do you take this prick
to be your husband? He ascendeth unto that state of extreme rapture,
the Seventh Heaven. Do Not Disterb. Now the pretentious fake
pretends he's never even heard of Asbury Park. Mr. Boils ascendeth
unto the empyrean of sophistication. Right. Mr. Boils chuckled at the
review by Miss Understand of Mr. Insight's newest novel, his third and,
surely, finest work. Eez zat ow she say? Le novel? Or eez eet le fiction?
Zat eez ow she say, Annie weez ze camera. You have, Dick, such a
strong face, I mean, fess. And so to bed. I don't know, baby, I don't
know, I think, I think I really *love* her. Who, Annie? Annie? No, not
Annie. I mean. Oh, of course, right, another Karen Fairgrounds, what
else? While I am but Mrs. Asbury Park, right, you rotten cheating
bastard? But God sees all from his altar, so when you embrace your
neighbor in the pew do not feel her up. She was always true to her high-
school sweetheart. It gets you right *here.* Rubbers and frayed collar
always looked at her underpants when she knelt to kiss the clammy
disgusting crucifix. And once she saw him touch himself with Sister
Mary Magdalene right there behind him. But she never told. She'll
never tell. Him and his boils, Christ! I thought we could play one of our
games, but these *boils.* I can hardly move. He'd be the priest and I
beneath my chaste Catholic wife and mother-of-four dress would wear
a red garter belt, black stockings. Bless me Father, for I have sinned,
I'm not wearing any underwear. My *child!* Dick was a desert boots
then. Dick was a faded denim jackets then. Dick was a button-down
collars then. Dick was a chilled white wine then. Dick was a I think I'll

take a cab then. Soon he forgot where Bath Beach was. *What* beach? Dick knew. But did he care? Neither did April, no more, no more. There was the stock boy and the mail boy and the shipping clerk and the UPS man and the trucker as well as the guy in the movies and the guy in the bar and that one and that one and that one and that one and that one. The seersucker suit wasn't really used to picking up girls, wife and children, the damn snapshots, Jesus, but he wanted to lick my little one, he called it. He loved his wife but oh! Is this any way for a good Catholic girl? Chicks really dig it when they try it. And though I washed my hands yet were they dirty. And though she ascendeth often yet was she as often laid. Dick knew, but.

Confitebor tibi in cithara . . . quare tristis es, anima mea, et quare conturbas me? . . . are we to blame her because try as she might she could not conceive? Not us. I sang the old songs and the new while Dick went on his artistic way. Have I mentioned his chain of Karens? But of course. Speak but the word and her soul shall be healed. What word is that? She won't cry anymore. They could have called him Charles or Peter, or her Melanie or Susan. Have another drink, no use talking about it. Don't neglect to give him his recorder or his guitar so that he can replace Bach's noise with his very own. Time out for tears. Well we don't have to worry about diaphragms or condoms or spermicidal foam, l'écume, l'écume des jours. That's what she should have had, a flower in her lung. Who asked for this? Just loved, loved the nights away. Oh what it seemed to be. Will we shake our heads because she performed fellatio on a number of men to whom she hadn't been properly introduced? Not us. That's the breaks. A couple of jiggers of moonlight, kid. Not too much ice. And add, say, a star. The brakeman fucked her, as did the conductor. I wanna be bad! The act of love, my dear woman, is primarily intended to insure the conception of. Oh for Christ sake give it a rest! Might as well shoot some Prell up there for all the good you do. Me? No, the janitor. Maybe I'd have had a snowman. When he's not near the girl he loves he'll take anything. I fall in love too easily. Why don't you play it on the recorder? If its name's Karen, instant erection. Make it a double, I should care. And the engineer came in his pants. On Fire Island I had the funny feeling that *maybe.* She can dream, can't she? I had the feeling that he had a feeling too that *maybe.* But they didn't even do it, he fell down the steps onto the sand and staggered into the night. She stood right there in the moonlight bare. Mine hostess, whose name I forget. What most disgusted her is that he didn't even take off his pants. Like the engineer. There they were like a couple of mongrels in the bushes. What was the old joke? Just hold the snake still? More truth than poetry in that. He got all red in the face and kicked the wall when he found out about me and poor hopeless Lou, in love in vain. Why didn't you kick the stereo, O reckless adventurer? The plastic-wrapped books? How come you didn't kick your gleaming rocking chair? You hypocrite, you *hypocrite!* Kick your desert boots, you bastard! Make me a Scotch, you bastard, a big one. And the wind blew up her nightie. How nice to have you and Dick for the weekend, her dazed Bryn Mawr eyes. She smiles and the angels sing. Sure, but it's too soon to know, sugar. He still doesn't believe me about Horace's as if I give a damn. I should have just pulled my clothes off, what the hell difference would it have made? Maybe that clubfooted pervert could have planted *his* seed. I'd have a little bastard born wearing a terrifying blue suit. Is it true what they say about Bunny? I wouldn't raise my boy to be a voyeur. Yes, I liked it, yes, I *did.* Yes, Lou is a joke. To *you.* Ow wondairfull eet eez zat you tek ze photograph? Stick it in your nose. I'd raise him up to be, I'd raise him up. Yes, she did that and she did that and she also did that and with him and him and them and somebody else and with her too. A lot of them. With their snapshots with their key-chains with their sad kinks with their interesting jobs and their mortgages and their cars falling apart and their wonderful kids and their understanding wives and their fake names. Uh, Bill, right, Bill, uh, Saunders. I love my wife, but. On my back on my knees standing up bending over naked half-dressed fully dressed on backseats balconies beaches booths dumb saloons motels stairwells bathrooms. Oh, you kid! What the hell did he care? Strangers in the night? Very witty, I'm surprised you knew I was gone. Go write another engaging story or whatever it is you write. Go see Karen Forage and cry on her compas-sionate shoulder. God, Dick, I just *wove* youw articwe it's just wike a beautifuw kind of wiwd enewgy. Isn't this Karen the sweet and under-standing one, very intelligent, loves opera, from the reaches of Terre Haute takes dictation types files cheerfully with her blue eyes on a better job or should I say career a general all-around wonderful girl with her little white blouse? with them there eyes? with simple jersey dress?

with businesslike mid-heel black pumps? with sweet little Alice-blue gown? Plus a college graduate! She takes him to paradise, but one mustn't forget the importance of the wine, perfectly chilled, with just a touch of petillance, the Brie, the crunchy baguette, the Gitanes, and the amusing vibrator. You sold your heart to the junkman, sweetie. That sly liar who just got out of the nuthouse then set his own house on fire, or something on fire, tells all, he had us both involved in you name it, anything and everything. Just said whatever came into his head to the cretin with the tape recorder. For what? A study of urban something, or the talk of the town. Does it matter that Dick and April were not what we were led to believe they were? Not to us. By the way, what were we led to believe? I'm goddamned if I know. But where there's smoke. I'll never be free. Couldn't stop talking, on and on. What a pair we were, according to Mr. Mouth, smoking, drinking, never thinking of tomorrow. Well, it makes the slobs feel better about their own quick journey to the grave, they are possessed of a deeper understanding. Of what? Of just what happens when. And also when. I've got my own troubles, let them play theirs down. The bastards. Dick thought the whole thing was funny. Hey, we're famous! Depressing. Pour me a glass of that Cabernet swill, the crap that Karen Peachy from the mountains and the prairies wuvs so much she could just dwink it *aw* up! But first, before you toast your love, a little head from the scintillant M.B.A. Am I right? So it's only nine in the morning. Sue me, should I be out jogging the pounds away? When he goes to sleep he never counts sheep he dreams about getting in Linda. Linda? What could have possessed my very own Mr. Denim to get himself involved with a non-Karen? You *are* a shrew! I only for Christ sake said hello to the girl. Fine, just don't bring home the Old Joe again, O.K.? Probably why she can't have any children, the mean filthy son of a bitch knowing he had it and not saying a word. Filthy? *Me,* filthy? After the rube with the foam-rubber dice on the rearview mirror wanted you to, you know. So what? *You* never seem to want my romancing. Very funny, very very funny. But it turned out that Linda was a pet name for, I'm not making this up, for Karen! Her father was a Buddy Clark fan, remember him? Oh sweet Jesus and all His wounds, spare me the grisly details of the *family.* But tell me, Karen-Linda, is her thing really made out of cellophane and ice cream? Jesus, you are really, really, Jesus. My sweet embraceable you, it's not your brain. I don't know what it is, I really can't explain. *Don't* explain! For Christ sake, give me a break! 'Twas then that he discovered Art. She can imagine him, oh, she often imagined him with Karen Pepsi Karen Heineken Karen Sperry. What's really so remarkable, Karen, is how he uses color itself as form. Alarums! Wow, Dick, I weawwy enjoyed that I weawwy fewt for the fiwst time that I can weawwy appweciate etcetewa etcetewa etcetewa. Oh oh oh oh oh! you beautiful doll! Then a bite of lunch, just a little lunch in a little restaurant on a little street in little old Greenwich Village, a charming place that Dick has loved for years, for a couple of months, since last week, he's never been there before. You hopeless chump. And soon after he buried us in Vermont, falling leaves, birches, God knows what, birds and bugs, neighbors with pale hatchet faces and transparent eyes whose forebears were whipped aboard ships at Portsmouth. The works. You know exactly what you can do with your clean air and your town meetings, don't you? Dick did not deign to reply. Deign this. His immaculate notebooks, his neat jottings, his ridiculous sharpened pencils, his Olivetti portable. All just so on a card table, Christ have mercy. Alone in the woods with that blank sheet of paper and without a sweetheart to his name. Does that view down to the river inspire you? There's nothing like nature, look at Thoreau. He thought he'd perhaps, *perhaps!* poach a salmon. Certainly, darling. In chocolate syrup, Fox's U-Bet? I am a bitch and why not, and why the hell not? My love for him meant. It meant heartaches. So who was it? So who took those goddamned pictures? Who? Did you get him hot, you whore? Did you change in front of him? Who was it? Did he fuck you, you whore? Say it isn't so, oh God, please. She smiled the smile she used to smile back in leafy Mechanicville. When she was sweet sixteen. I won't tell. I don't see me in his eyes anymore. I never told. It's a sin to tell a lie. The blood streaks the beatifically suffering face of Our Lady. He did hate to lose his favorite niece, oh that's O.K., plenty of others around, Uncle Johnny, thank heaven for little girls, right? There he stood in his cheap rental tux. Received every Sunday with all his cronies and their dopey wives. My mother used to say, you'll pardon the expression, April, but my ass would make a Sunday face for all of them. There is most definitely a curse on your families and it fell on you, oh you're ugly. Beans, carrots, radishes, God knows what. All failed. Couldn't grow a marigold. He wanted to go in and see

Saul or Sol, God, I can't remember those wretched men, to talk about some changes in the first part. Certainly, you must see to the particulars of your Art. If they asked you, could you write a book? There's no *living* with you. So? Go live with Karen whoever. Thertainly, Dick, pwease come up to my pwace and I'ww make you some bacon and eggs. Why, what a cute little apron. Do you wike it? And those wonderful postcard reproductions in the bathroom! I got them fwom the Museum of Modewn Art. Wonderful! Did you see the marvelous retrospective of anybody last year? *Did* she? It was marvewous! And in a trice he had his fly open, you can bet on it. Just a prisoner of love, poor baby, my wife won't *let* me. Did you have a good time in the dynamic, vibrant, ever-changing, restless, and, how shall I put it, *electric* city? Did you have any interesting conversations? Take in any of the *great* shows? Run into Karen Millpond who never never *thaw* one ath big ath yours? You're drunk as shit. Have you noticed how all the really exciting people there carry attaché cases and take cabs? From their lofts to other people's lofts? You're drunk. Glittering crowds in canyons of steel, all from Nebraska. All the Karens. She couldn't help mentioning the Karens, could she? You're drunk, go to bed. Yes, you son of a bitch, and I'm going to get drunker. How's the *stuff* coming, what's the title again, *Blackhead*? She should care what she said. Do we care? Not us. Dick knew, but did Dick care? You walk along the street of sorrow, Don Juan, right? Or is it the boulevard of broken dreams? My God! Is that a pimple on your sensitive and aesthetic face? Don't worry about it, all right? Do me a favor. I love how your eyes are fixed on the trees. In Southern fiction they call that the tree line, don't they, Massa? Shut up. Don't you love Southern fiction, so earthy, so natural, so attuned to the art of narrative, and yet, so, so, so deep. Shut up. Do you know why this is the case? Shut up. I'll tell you why, I'll tell you, you pitiful sterile bastard with your well-wrought crap, because *all* Southern writers had a mother or a grandmother or an aunt or some other wise old person who told them the most *fascinating* stories in their youth. Usually on the old porch. Shut up. Or the old verandah. Shut shut up! Under the Spanish moss. For *Christ* sake! That's why they can write those rattling good tales, stories so full of life that make you understand life and everything. She's going to make another pitcher of martinis because she doesn't know about him but she, for one, is goddamned sick and tired of swinging on the goddamned birches. Can I get you a mason jar full of white lightning, darling? Or is it just plain corn? Earthy? Electrifying? Full of dusty red clay roads and tree lines and overalls? Will you please shut the hell up? That sounded just like dialogue! Do you want to know why Southern writers write such great dialogue? Jesus! Because in the South, wait a minute! Because in the South, everybody *really* talks! I mean they don't just talk, they *talk*. Don't you think it's a lost art? Don't you think that television is to blame? Don't you? Oh, God, my heart cries for him. We used to go to all the very gay places. Who cares? Not *us*. Now we have all these friends and a lot of parties. I'll go to bed with anybody I want, I'm still good enough to get somebody. Those come-what-may places. And. And. Why am I so? Sad. It's the feel of life. I hope you're satisfied. That first time I took off my clothes he blushed, he turned his eyes away. Now he eats breakfast and lunch in his studio. *Studio,* my God. In the mirror her face looked like Our Lady's. Whose blessed eyes bleed for all the sins of the world. Girls, the blood streaming down is because. I remember all their faces if not their names. The blood streams because. Yes, girls. Bloody sanitary napkins, bloody tampons, blood, blood, always plenty of goddamned blood. I don't think I've ever missed a period, and does it matter whose fault it was? Not to us. Down. Down and down. Lost April, the heart within her died.

Payer of stayers

to a loft, a beach, a field

Said fine O.K. when asked to marry went down to the bar drank
bourbon draft beer played Billie "No Regrets" over over over Harlan
came limped with strange tall woman dead eyes black metallic dress:
was on the roof locked out on a bitter cold night: no paint turpentine
canvas paper food money nothing but a pint of Dixie Belle half a fifth of
Majorska: a smaller painting crimson Prussian blue imitation of
Guston *The Raid* said was best work so far Jesus Christ! let's face it!
hypnotized by self-pity: asked take off everything but boots what did
care: large eerie painting black vertical slash in center said it was death:
climbed stairs loft behind looked up skirt: told about Harlan New
Mexico looked and nodded: walked upstairs alone again again walked
downstairs alone again again: hateful couple Lou and Sheila somebody
on landing too listened cursed kicked bottles around behind door:
looked at two ears of Indian corn over stove asked if never for Christ
sake heard of Popeye: put cap on head fucked from behind: answered
phone said no said no said all right yes got drunk walked across town
upstairs undressed: wouldn't show one photograph managed to steal
sheriff and wife: ripped *The Raid* across with beer-can opener wept
chanted Guston Guston Guston: called Lucy Taylor came over helped
down with suitcases: told again about Harlan New Mexico heroin
others photographs looked again nodded again: hit with belt over and
over came on the floor wanted to vomit got excited: screamed about
white linen dress white sandals hair screamed all the way downstairs:
slammed front door: second night brought two pencil drawings stared
puzzled the bastard: yelled yelled again waited yelled again window
opened key in Milky Way wrapper: tried to arouse failed tried failed:
cried went downstairs got drunk: went upstairs drunk: cried tried to

27

arouse failed: put cap on looked out window while slept: harsh thin smell turpentine sun curtainless window on death: Lucy helped upstairs with suitcases frowned filth broken walls ceilings must be some fantastic lay to put up with this: lit cigarettes don't know what:

went back in dead of winter married thank God alone looked grey sea going out: should have known first night around eight oh Jesus we're going to run out of booze Jesus Christ might as well have kept my clothes on: asked as joke about my past some joke left Harlan out of it Midwest puritanical questions: yet took my hand small canvas white yellow peach softest violet *Joanne's White*: no matter how no matter couldn't keep him hard lay in sand wept apologized cursed moaned: at the top of the steps to beach still calm low tide hand in hand walked all right: asked me why I wanted photograph innocence white pants white shirt white tennis shoes smiled in sun glare Kansas City sun through windows innocence how come you: rain pelted ran upstairs kerosene heater tomato soup rice beans franks salad stripped fucked kneeling came and came oh he came kneeling sweet cunt sweet sweet cunt groaned like dirty books: wanted to know wanted really about Harlan smoked cigarette after cigarette I brought up I told Joanie Teddy Marlene all Chester Max oh Jesus all the O'Neills Connie all every damn one couldn't shut up made some up all: fire: ocean just visible moonlight: why: why why: but why: followed me to beach his hand cupped between my legs: why oh Jesus why: drank cursed yelled argued red face vicious: *Joanne's White* is phony phony piece of phony shit dumb fucking bitch whore: vicious: worse and worse: worse and worse and worse: impossible: hid Mom's handmade birthday card beloved girl my sweet child of August: hung over fragile read me Hart Crane wet thick wind slicing through the blanket: another miraculous palest yellow white lavender fuchsia green size of a postcard *Provincetown Alba* absolutely beautiful: for you: for me: for you forgive me: card from Lucy we all miss you sweet Bunny hurry home looked at me the card this the ugly fucking dike you told me about?: pushed me right down the steps skinned my knee forearm now bullshit me about your tough life lit a cigarette: raw clams baked clams clam soup basil thyme white wine fresh tomatoes who says I'm not a good provider fucked me my white sundress sandals sweet breeze: on the deck sketched me over and over threw everything away I don't even understand your goddamned blank wasp face: the last night stupid movie argument about where oh God about where it was filmed in a rage cursing at me I wouldn't he masturbated in front of me see? see? see this goddamn you?: Tania came with some man talked nonstop gossip to be married like marrying a radio we laughed afterward shh they'll hear us: a canvas board three brushes his paints give it a try don't worry about it give it a try don't be nervous see how the paint feels: stopped talking about books he hated those he hadn't read but wouldn't read you and your Symbolist fags: in Truro middle-aged man limped I stopped I must have gone white looked at me his face I must have gone: New Mexico: I told him contempt rage you can't paint you can't write you can't cook make the bed can't sweep the floor do the dishes can't do anything can't fuck right you're killing me! you're killing me opened a gallon of white port: killed me fucking already can't even paint anymore worth a damn look at this shit!: and kicked *Joanne's White* across the room:

bores me to death: empty stadium: hand on my hip: talks about quarterbacks: hand on my breast: down the stairs: talks about Ohio: almost puts me to sleep: Caddy and Quentin: under the stands: takes bra off opens pants I can't look do it to him with my hand: comes all over me my skirt: up the stairs: he loves me: he bores me to: leaves me at the bus stop: walk back to stadium empty sky: sit on the grass: throw up: stiff stain: walk up the stairs: sky empty:

to an inn, a school, a front door

Biff Harlan Harlan and Biff Harlan and Teddy Harlan and Biff and Teddy Harlan and Joanie and Teddy Joanie and Teddy and Marlene and Harlan Joanie and Sam and Biff and Harlan Marlene and Terri and Georgette and Harlan Marlene and Biff and Harlan Dolores and Marlene and Harlan Biff Harlan and Biff Harlan Dolores and Liz and Chester and Max and Harlan Chester and José and Harlan Ed and Kate O'Neill and Harlan Kate O'Neill and Harlan Ricardo and Ed O'Neill and Harlan Harlan Harlan Harlan and Biff George and Connie and the O'Neills and Louie and Harlan Harlan April and Johnny and Harlan: all preserved forever: clear glossy images:

good-looking beard will for me top step Art Students': will be *Fruits and Dross* or *Pistachio Oval* evoke sneers laughter: have incredible body when sketch again and again erection: limited talents commercial bent: son of a bitch: wait for me every day drunk or sober bottom of stairs: look up skirt step stool my paint box my apron: climb down step stool hands hips hands thighs sneaky bastard dirty as if he: will cross-eyed artistic psychologist or goddamn schoolteacher brushing up against me: take a break: relax: step stool my legs: he'll throw cap out window he'll vomit on floor model somebody's canvas: that look on that cold face that cold look when Harlan this when Harlan that: frightened girl from Akron or some place kiss feel breasts why not? between landings: water color six ladders to a sky azure *New Mexico Blooze*: not bad: admirable talents small but fine: the beard hand on my ass in the dark street a drink? a bite to eat?: run down scattering charcoal pencils brushes everything: he'll incoherent mumble steps to the creative tequila in a pickle jar sweat running down face: creative bitch!: *Fruits and* laugh spit on it what a piece of garbage: start on beard in basement his eyes ohh good and stiff he'll ohh baby: Harlan dream naked club-foot naked clubfoot in between his legs: Agfa apron beard say they can't see your pure and eccentric but real downstairs Rocky's Tavern what the hell: really I mean really beard will say real talent I'll settle myself legs open as if by: he'll fall front steps or something down the street he'll break wrist he'll break again: beard at step stool when I'll get down he'll smirk love really love your ice-blue I'll blush I'll: my father? my father will come upstairs puffing oh God the tweed jacket the blue denim shirt *The Nation* in his ripped pocket he'll smile: so what's up with you?: he'll say can't paint worth a shit a good goddamn who the fuck do I think I'm kidding this *New Mexico* crap for Christ's sake good for the Salvation Army or your dumb old man for Christ he'll go down to the ball game cursing and laughing he'll:

be the father open your arms smile at the top of the Christmas stairs: be the tweed jacket always be that be that good teacher: be the beautiful dreamer: peach silk slip on a holiday visit: Lucy will show me Lucy will take off our bras: holiday dinner a little wine the trees pale in the grey mist low clouds: elbow patches blue work shirts he can carve he can cut the pies: like the watercolor: after snowstorm he shovels a tunnel to the door he takes a little Scotch neat his face all red her jack-o'-lanterns beautifully made each one a different face his deprived underprivileged her Indian corn her tableware ceramics and clay the porch steps: her dress molds to her buttocks and they are and they are this is how daddy sees her: weeping in my room: pumpkins autumn my birthdays and theirs Christmas Ralph comes over the same bore the same football: pale leaves in mist: I'll never again daddy be what I what I did the men and the women the sheriff and his wife the redneck truck drivers the married couple and the cameras Harlan never daddy not Kate's thing she straps on never I'll be the cover girl in white again: the plaid skirt the knee socks white blouse I'll be again what was: he'll be gone he'll be dead the filthy pig his filthy clubfoot dead: be the girl who showers in the bathroom with the pink roses and blue baskets calmly diagonal: be the colored lights and the ribbons and the tattered Santa Claus the turkey sober small jokes: the dishes and mom in her navy blue woolen dress her black pumps and be the daddy in the repp stripe tie and the pie and some cognac: and mom of course your mother has put on a little weight: but in he smiles but in the right places: we will love we'll mom and daddy love love: smile: smiles: they smile at the top of the front steps love: be love no big thing just easy and easy love: just some decent love for God's sake: be the father and mother: be that.

Cage

Anne Kaufman née Marshall: born to Jude Marshall, an alcoholic crew chief for the telephone company, and Tessie Blankenship Marshall, the only one of four children to be placed in an orphanage by her deserted mother. State Teachers College, where she excels in athletics. Extremely popular member of the Christian Student Union. That's a good one. Full skirts. Peasant blouses. Hair in a thick yellow braid, bright and glowing Scots-Irish face. Etcetera. Smell of Castile soap. Pots, ceramics, weaving, knitting, crocheting. Competent cook. White kitchen curtains, yellow-daisies print. Bakes whole-grain bread, literary ambitions. Too good to be true. However. New York at twenty-two, job at Black Ladder Bookshop. Meets Thelma Kruliciewicz and startles herself by having a brief affair with her while living with Karen Ostrom. Make it a passionate affair. Meets Lee "ZuZu" Jefferson, gets job as editorial assistant at *Hip Vox*, where Lee works. Lee isn't a bad name. Buys new clothes, has hair cut, meets Guy Lewis and Joanne Harley. Correction: Joanne Ward. Moves into Guy's loft. Marries Guy one month later in civil ceremony. Oh boy. Has affair with Olga Begone, a mythocentric poet, cross-eyed to boot. Moves in with Olga, divorces Guy. [Two-year lacuna.] Tessie dies, Jude remarries the owner of the Naughtie Nightie boutique in Kirkwood, Missouri, Charlotte Pugh. Small world. Anne appears at wedding, held on Charlotte's yacht in Palm Beach. Ridiculous! All right, Biscayne Bay. Ridiculous! Anne gets drunk, confides to Ralph Ingeman, a childhood friend who now sports an ill-fitting toupee, that Jude sexually molested her for years and that for Ralph's information she isn't wearing any underclothes. He confesses his long-standing and hopeless love for her. She wonders if he'd like her to prove it by standing against the sunlight coming in through the bay window. The porthole. Returns to New York, attends art school, shows no talent. Attends poetry workshop. Curious word.

Learns to write poems in imitation of Theodore Roethke. Publishes "Snails" in *Lorzu,* a little magazine edited by Craig Garf and ZuZu. Ambience? Literary. Sniggering helps nothing. Moves out of small Brooklyn Heights apartment owing three months' rent. So much for the magical fucking skyline. Moves in with Craig Garf and begins to do his typing. Etcetera. Meets Vance Whitestone and Dick Detective, known to some as "the priest." White wine. Sazeracs. Vodka with cranberry juice. And so on. Fun-filled days and thrilling evenings. Right. Has affair with April Detective, an enthusiastic bisexual. Jude dies in fall from telephone pole in Corfu. Something odd there. Charlotte Pugh returns to Lawton, Oklahoma, after selling boutique to Phyllis Redding, an Englishwoman with an obscure past. Small world. Anne meets Leo Kaufman, a poet, moves out of Craig's apartment and into Leo's. Too good to be true. However. He enchants her by claiming that the trash and garbage that fill the shotgun flat on Avenue D is "dirt that blew in through the windows." White kitchen curtains, make it a cherries-and-leaves print. Writes Theodore Roethke but the famed poet does not deign to reply. Close call! *Very* attractive stationery. Craig gives her a number of informal lectures on the enchanted world of books and she gradually begins to understand truly the wonder and delight of. Hold it. Leo asks her to wear a diaper to satisfy a common sexual taste. Some dish, he later says to a stranger in a saloon in Teaneck. Wrong town. Anne and Leo are married, have a wedding supper at Stanziani's. No. Fugazi's. No. Imbriale's. No. Some Italian joint with a beer garden in the back, spaghetti, paper lanterns. Those Italians. They return to a burglarized apartment, in the middle of which are two fresh turds. My God. Correction: In the middle of which is a note on Anne's very attractive stationery that reads "thaks four the Mikky ways." Something odd there. They speak quietly of Freud, excrement, and money, but Leo cries anyway. There's no winning. Anne sits at the window listening to the screams and curses of the dis-possessed floating through the courtyard, echoing again and again, maddeningly, despairingly, bringing her at last face-to-face with the hollow travesty. Hold it. Anne sits at the window smoking. Make it nervously smoking. Nervously chain-smoking. Leo writes "The Burglary," a kind of sirventes. Check word. Leo reads the poem to Anne and then says, for no apparent reason, that his occasional

impotence can be remedied if she will allow him to spank her. That's a
good one. If she will spank him. Oh boy. How about with a belt? Something odd there. Anne remembers that she once told Ralph Ingeman, or
so she tells Leo, that she wanted a word with him out in the hayloft,
preferably naked. In Biscayne Bay. Biscayne Bay? Leo queries. Wrong
place. Anne accedes to Leo's perverse desires, formed quite some time
before. That's the way it goes. Anne begins keeping a journal that
meticulously records their erotic life together. You never know. Leo
begins to drink heavily and purchases several recordings of Civil War
songs of the Union Army, which he plays while drinking muscatel and
A & P Tudor beer. Check brand name. He tells Anne that he wishes he
were dead since he's dead anyway. Disturbing yet quintessentially
melodramatic. Anne gives the ice-blue panties that he buys for her as a
peace offering to the super's wife, Frieda Canula, who puts them on her
head to scrub the stairs. So much for exotic lingerie among our
Albanian friends. Anne spends an evening smoking marijuana with the
Detectives and all three go to bed together. She tries a few things, some
of which are good and some all right. Others won't work because of the
physical limitations of the human body. So the manuals were wrong!
That's the way it goes. But give her credit, give her credit. That's a good
one. Leo frequents the Soirée Intime and becomes enamored of Léonie
Aubois, who always laughs at him and rarely fails to tell him to get a
haircut. Why? asks Leo, peering out from the vast bush that encircles
his head. Always the card. Anne shows her journal to ZuZu, now the
managing editor of *Hip Vox.* ZuZu decides to publish excerpts from it
anonymously. Anne buys a fedora and pickets the offices of Crescent
and Chattaway, publishers of *Suck My Whip, Lace Me Tighter, Joys
of the Square Knot,* and other works of the erotic imagination. Correction: other filthy and degrading trash! Leo begins writing *Isolate
Flecks,* a roman à clef whose most reprehensible character is named
Annie Sheriff. These writers. He uses Anne's journal as a source,
although how he managed to. Hold it. Anne moves in with Vance
Whitestone and Leo somehow meets a young woman named Ellen
Marowitz. The narrative quickens. Now we're beginning to see
daylight. Anne closes their joint bank account and gives the money to
Vance. She begins wearing burlap skirts, sandals, and tattered T-shirts
and stops shaving her legs and underarms. God knows why. Vance

introduces her to Tony Lamont, author of *Synthetic Ink,* who is aroused by her hairiness and pursues her sporadically but unsuccessfully. Leo meets her in the street one day and tells her that he wants a divorce, that he is finally beginning to *live,* and that he is rewriting the poems of Dante Gabriel Rossetti as free verse. Wow. Anne tells him that it's fine with her, that he's as crazy as he ever was, and, on parting, that she isn't wearing any underclothes. Search me. She begins an affair with Tony Lamont, moves out of Vance's apartment when she finds Karen Ostrom's blouse in the closet and her bean sprouts in the refrigerator, then moves in with Tony. [Two-month lacuna.] She meets Lorna Flambeaux, author of *The Sweat of Love,* and they have a brief affair. An intense affair. A brief, intense, and torrid affair. On their one-month anniversary, she gives Lorna her fedora, and Lorna, in turn, buys her a pair of Sweet-Orr overalls. How fetching she looks! Fetching? Anne discovers that she has the manuscript of Leo's first story, "Sleeping with the Lions," and burns it in order to destroy not only the mere physical object but the outward symbol of a love that at one time burned as. Hold it. Meets Annette Lorpailleur, who wants to arrange to have photographs of her taken in what she calls interesting bohemian poses. Oh boy. Anne goes to a Halloween costume party at Horace Rosette's, dressed in a diaper, bra, and high heels, and even though she's crying on the inside, Rupert Whytte-Blorenge steals her shoes. Henri Kink, a failed novelist, commits suicide after writing the screenplay for *Hellions in Hosiery.* His farewell note reads "Enough is enough!" Always the card. At his funeral, Anne meets Ann Taylor Redding and Ellen Marowitz, the latter clinging to Leo's arm, and to whom Anne subsequently refers as Miss Eskimo Pie, Miss Golden Delicious, and Miss Popsicle. So much for remaining good friends. Jack Marowitz, Ellen's brother, whose professional name is Jackie Moline, propositions Anne, offering her three-hundred dollars if she will perform a rather reprehensible sex act with him and she accepts. You never can tell. Anne begins to affect severe tailored suits, crisp blouses, low-heeled shoes, has her hair styled in a loose chignon. Check word. She considers converting to Roman Catholicism but is discouraged when she discovers that Annie Flammard, the star of *Hellions in Hosiery,* was once a Sister of Charity. Small world. Anne is duped into going to bed with Barnett Tete, a wealthy businessman, who has not been able to get her out of his mind since seeing her at Horace Rosette's Christmas party. Wrong occasion. Her divorce from Leo becomes final and she precipitately marries Barnett, who insists that she live alone for most of the year in his Biscayne Bay mansion. Aha! She cuts her hair short and buys a wardrobe of pink sleeveless dresses in the hope of catching the eye of a plain, no-nonsense, good-hearted man, but succeeds only in attracting the attention of a vacationing professor, who, it turns out, thinks that pink makes a woman look helpless. These academics. The gardener, Reeve, makes her pregnant and for a lark she blames the professor, who swiftly returns to his sylvan, wooded campus in the Mississippi swamps. She has an abortion and as she leaves the clinic is struck a vicious blow with a picket sign carried by Phyllis Redding, who now makes her home in North Miami and works as a clerk in the Tropical Bible Aids Shoppe just outside of town. Ridiculous. [Three-year lacuna.] Anne appears as Sister Philomena Veronica in *Sisters in Shame,* a low-budget horror movie. So much for the religious impulse. Phyllis Redding is seduced by a stock clerk at the Born Again Employees' Picnic, after which she writes an article for the magazine *Jesus!,* "The Horror of My Forced Abortion," which she dedicates "to my unborn Robin, who will never feel the humidity on his little face." Whew. A death notice for an "Anne Kaufman" appears in *The Sacramento Bee.* Wrong Anne. Wrong paper. Anne returns to New York, her name changed to Anne Leo, determined to make a go of it in business, but fails to interest employers in her eclectic experience and life skills. So much for the cheery fucking magazine articles she's been reading. Barnett Tete announces that he can make gold, calm storms, and raise the dead, and is committed to a mental hospital by Rupert Whytte-Blorenge, who has earlier been named by Barnett as attorney-in-fact for the purposes of executing durable general power of attorney for health care of Barnett. That's a good one. Anne moves in with Rupert, who now owns a chain of shoe stores. Too good to be true. [Six-year lacuna.] Anne buys out White Sun Talent Associates, Inc., and begins producing educational films for the Golden Rose Fellowship, an organization whose energies are directed primarily against public restrooms as places of sin. These crusaders. Marries Chet Kendrick, a former actor, now a Neo-Neo-Humanist with a syndicated newspaper column of conservative views entitled "I Got Mine." She presides over licentious Washington parties to which high government officials are invited and records their unruly behavior on videotape. You never know. Travels to Mexico, has cosmetic surgery, invests in La Basurita Aztec Food Products, Inc., and two years later moves to Switzerland, where she begins work on her memoirs, *Perfumes of Arabia,* with the assistance of Leo Kaufman, a more-or-less permanent guest in her chalet. So much for burning the old fucking bridges.

Cusine this and cuisine that, you know, the half-raw carrots and the lumpy mashed potatoes, salads swimming in oil with those massive chunks of blue cheese, or bleu cheese, or cheese bleu, lots of luck, but you know, Miss Eskimo Pie, Miss Milky Way, Miss Tutti-Frutti, she doesn't really like Leo to spank her but after a while it isn't so bad and then, you know, Ellen sort of gets to sort of like it, she likes everything about Leo, my God, even though her old man, Jack, doesn't like him much, or her brother, Jackie, that gorilla, he doesn't like him at all, he thinks, they think, he's a pervert and a schnorrer, a sort of well, you know, a faggot, that's Jackie's word, their word, you know, too bad, of course, the cocktail dresses, sweet Jesus, pink, baby blue, lavender, fuchsia, pale yellow, you name it and if it's cute, well, there it is, plain black high-heeled pumps, Peck and Peck cardigans and blouses, Harris tweed jackets, pleated skirts, just a picture of restrained perfection, Barnard and Sarah Lawrence too, you know, best friend Elizabeth Reese, prize-winning student poet, Jesus Christ, her "Starry Night, Bronxville: With Orgasm" creates a small scandal because the "Helene" of the poem, whose "shining head moved in / gentle pulse be- / tween my joyous thighs" is thought to be, well, you know, thought to be Ellen, too bad, that's at Bennington, so what all the fuss is about, God knows, you know, she doesn't really like to, you know, do it with Elizabeth, but after a while it isn't so bad, she likes Bennington, except for Jane Richardson, who is always, you know, always the old families and the old houses and the old estates and the old who the fuck knows, the old *Mayflower,* and the feeling is sort of, well, mutual, there is that snub nose and those good clothes and that creamy complexion, but, you know, to old Jane she's just a new kike, you know how those old girls can be, the story goes that old Jane gets the old Joe from a sleaze rock-

and-roll drummer and that her sister, Punkie, those names will murder you, she runs off with a Cuban-Irish truck driver with a few tattoos, you know, some guy who delivers firewood or manure or whatever to the old summer place at the old seashore, and has a bastard son, so the two old girls liven up that watery blood, you know, that old blood, too bad, but we are off course, Jesus Christ, Elizabeth moves to New York, no, Elizabeth more or less disappears, so what, Ellen moves back to New York to her parents' house, time flies, she gets a job, the Marvelous Magazine Management Corporation, publishers of *Action, Men's Action, True Action, Action Monthly, Jungle Action, Action at Sea, Sports Action, Hot Action, Actionworld, Universe of Action, War Action, Guns in Action,* and other real men's magazines, on the strength of her education, right, her résumé, her crossed legs, you know, her wide dark eyes, her, well, sort of eager look, her engaging curiosity, Jesus Christ, her crossed legs, you know, people die, as usual, then many more die, too bad, Ellen lives, Greenwich Village, wooden spatulas, wooden spoons, wooden bowls, wooden breadboards, all-purpose wine glasses, ceramic this, ceramic that, a leather address book, some, you know, attractive and unusual prints, a fucking brick wall, more wooden things, Jesus Christ, Lincoln Center, you know, right, she meets ZuZu Jefferson, an editor at Crescent and Chattaway, and is soon, you know, in the thick of things, Jesus Christ, at a party, you know, one of those parties, where one might meet daring editors and writers in touch with their generation, and fascinating artistic people of, you know, all sorts, including the deadbeat who just got an appointment to, you know, teach something somewhere, no, to be a, you know, writer in residence, right, and Barnett Tete is there, some strange girl with an accent, no, some strange girl, a deaf mute or some-thing, a cripple, something, she just, you know, just sort of pulls her panties off while she's dancing, some novelist, Cecil something, he just sort of pukes in a corner, pisses in the bathtub, throws the baked ham out the window, a barrel of laughs, a real artist, and Ellen meets, well, you know, not meets, but talks a little to Annie Flammard, who does something, something having to do with, you know, art, in advertising, Jesus Christ, and through Annie she meets, she is introduced to, Leo Kaufman, a poet, *The Beautiful Sun,* acclaimed by those few who know, and Leo is working on a new long poem, political but not, you

know, overtly so, not propaganda, so he says, wild mop of hair, you
know, he's afraid of the barber, don't ask, ninety-eight-cent tie with
grease stains, rumpled suit, shoes, well, Jesus Christ, unbelievable, she
doesn't really like him to spank her, you know, too damn bad, Leo sort
of, well, he puts his hand right between her legs, a real bard, they're at
the table with the baked ham, no, that's on the sidewalk, the roast
turkey, the cold cuts, no, actually, they're at the table with the booze,
the bowl of melted ice cubes, and Ellen, well, you know, there she is in
her pink cocktail dress, Ellen is sort of, well, stunned, Craig Garf, a
handsome man, prematurely grey, you know, no, balding with greying
sideburns, no, rather fat and he seems to wheeze, well, Craig takes her
hand and leads her away from Leo's hand, and Anne, Leo's first wife,
no, his wife, right, they're still married, Anne comes up to Leo and slaps
him across the face and Jack Towne, somebody, probably Jack, you
know, he takes Ellen into a bedroom and this comes to that, you know,
whatever, when Ellen gets home she's missing her underwear, except
for her slip, which is torn, she's wearing a grey fedora too big for her,
right, her skirt has stiff stains all over it, you know, a Peck and Peck, no,
a Bergdorf's, who knows, it has these stains on the unearthly purple
material, no, blue, no, aqua, no, turquoise, no, it's pink, stains on her
pink skirt, dress, a garment not too particularly chic, but Ellen has an
idea about herself, don't ask, Jack Towne calls up, but no dice, too bad,
he really would like to get to know, you know, get to know her better,
right, legs, right, thighs, right, you know, she really interests him a lot,
you know, more people die, on and on it goes, that's the way, you know,
then it's Thanksgiving yet again, Jesus Christ, time flies, Anne and Leo
Kaufman, Sazeracs, turkey, range turkey, Jesus Christ, ZuZu, Craig, a
fruity chablis, Vance Whitestone, Karen Ostrom with, you know, an
organic plum pudding without anything at all in it, amazing, Jesus
Christ, some priest, right, a regular guy, right, all-natural hashish, no,
he's an ex-priest, expresso and cognac, Ellen and the ex-priest and
somebody else in a closet, somebody, but, you know, who cares, some
pills, some capsules, lots of cognac, this and that and things happen,
things happen, Henri Kink comes for after-dinner drinks, with a striking
tall woman with icy, well, blank eyes, beautiful legs, she's in a black
metallic dress, her voice is, well, you know, her voice is, well, uncanny,
Jesus Christ, and a third guest, a clubfooted man, he rubs against Ellen

rudely in the kitchen, she's getting ice, he, you know, he is really very rude, very, you know, bold, she can feel his erection against her thigh, she can see it inside his, Jesus Christ, he's wearing these pants, this suit, he's got on this weird blue suit, it is really, you know, very, very, you know, it is odd indeed, he just rubs again, Jesus Christ, she gets back to the living room, dimly lit, her living room, the ex-priest, you know, the one in the closet with somebody else, time flies, that was two years ago, time flies, you know, it just, right, she notices that her skirt is somehow up, she is not quite there at all, she is, well, you know, stoned, she notices, too, that there seems to be a head between her thighs, it's the ex-priest, he's, right, Jesus Christ, and there's the creep, the weasel, the man with the suit, the clubfoot, the insane blue thing, he's in a chair with a camera, Jesus Christ, his eerie pants are, well, they're, well, he's opened them, well, you know, she lies back, her eyes close, she, you know, who cares, soon Ellen goes to Switzerland, no, Brazil, no, Milan, no, she goes to, she goes to, you know, she goes to work, right, to work, she gets fired, work, fired, and so on, she gets a job through Jackie, he calls himself Jackie Moline, he owns a couple of saloons, Cadillac Lounge, Reno Tavern, Gold Coast Bar and Grill, he has money on, you know, he has money out on the street, he's prematurely bald, greying sideburns, no, a little overweight, no, he's got distinguished prematurely grey hair, no, silver, he gets a job for her at one of the, right, the Foxhead Inn, a cocktail waitress, you know, those legs, her unabashed curiosity, right, those legs, short flared skirts, legs, thighs, black mesh stockings, no, she works as a hostess, svelte, sophisticated, some drinking, right, some coke, right, a little hash, a little this, nothing serious, a little that, she meets Barry Gatto, pieces of Mu-Shu pork stuck between his front teeth, disgusting, too bad, a Long Island drive-in movie, *Silk Thighs,* Ellen with the ex-priest, Frank Baylor, right, that's his name, and what with this and what with that, he asks her to, well, he doesn't really ask her, he says that he can't bear to look at her and not, well, you know, tiny flared skirt, legs, thighs, svelte, whatever, he says he can't bear, well, he can't, and so Ellen says, well, she doesn't say, who cares, and more die, time keeps, you know, it keeps passing, Lincoln Center, the ballet, Lincoln Gom, ecology, politics, Buddhism as transcendent xenophobia, Jesus Christ, and Leo, one night, he's drunk, he's always drunk, too bad, Leo asks her to come with him to his apartment one night, right, after the bars close, no, just before they close, she is celebrating her birthday, dinner with Jack and Jackie, you know, family ties are, you know, her mother isn't there, her mother is, well, dead, Leo asks her to, will she please, he loves her, Leo loves her, Jesus Christ, he looks at her, her legs, you know, her thighs, well, you know, she goes with him to his apartment, she looks at things, Jesus Christ, beer cans, beer bottles, soda cans, stacks of magazines and newspapers, shirt cardboards, filthy piles of clothes, no, piles of filthy clothes, the sink crammed with greasy dishes, hordes of cockroaches, the mousetrap with the putrefacting mouse in it, the broken refrigerator, smell of freezone, in it a half-quart of Majorska vodka and a washcloth stained with blood, Jesus Christ, the clogged toilet, grimy towels, smudged glasses, food-encrusted stove, the mattress on the floor, grey, stained sheets, a pair of torn beige panties in a corner, pornographic magazines, *Nylon Pussies, Whores in Heels, Anal Fancies,* stained with, well, soap covered with strands of hair, foul toothbrush, hairbrush, comb, razor, broken-legged table littered with God knows what, Olivetti portable, half-ream of yellow second sheets, loose stamps, correspondence, paperback mysteries, science fiction, *New World Dictionary,* pens and pencils, dull paring knife, rotted apple, overflowing ashtray, five or six crumpled Camel packages, a brown-stained butt glued to a spot of dried beer, half-full quart jug of Gallo Burgundy, envelopes, notepads, a spiral-bound notebook, three Trojan condoms, Jesus Christ, enough, Ellen takes her clothes off, you know, carefully, kneels on the mattress, you know, gingerly, no, Leo asks her to put her heels back on, he, you know, he hands her his belt, he kneels on the mattress, she doesn't really, but, you know, he starts to beg, you know, Jesus Christ, she tells Jackie, no, she tells Jack and Jack tells Jackie, no, she tells them both, separately, she and Leo, she tells them, are, you know, they're sort of, well, married, my God, Jackie finds Leo, he, you know, he sort of hits him, he sort of socks him in the nose, well, in the jaw, he whacks him, you know, a little, in the eye too, he, well, he beats the shit out of Leo, he calls him a pervert, then Ellen buys him leather notebooks for his jottings, for his, you know, his notes, so that he won't, you know, lose any ideas, Jesus Christ, Anne, well, Anne is a bitch, Leo says, you know, Anne is some bitch, what else is new, Leo goes on and on, daily, nightly, Ellen would rather that he just didn't get so, you know, so, so, Leo goes on, Anne, she turns out to be, among other things, a, you know, a motherfucking cuntlapping dike whore of a shit-eating titlicking cunt, whew, Ellen meets Olga Begone, you know, author of *Man-Kill* and *Nutless!*, and, you know, Anne and Olga are, at this time, whatever that may mean, they're sort of, you know, living together, then she's introduced to Lorna Flambeaux, whose latest book is, right, *Leaves of Yearning*, an imaginary journey through the mind of Renée-Pélagie, and then she sort of meets Roberte Flambeaux, the chairmistress of the Daughters of Durga, and the author of various tracts and, well, you know, manifestoes, and when Leo makes Anne into a monster in *Isolate Flecks*, Ellen, well, Ellen, you know, Ellen is angry, you know, because now, well, time passes, more deaths, Leo spanks Ellen, he paddles her with a Hi-Lo bat, he makes her wear her pink sleeveless dress because, he says, oh boy, it makes her look like a whore pretending to be a virgin, Jesus Christ, there is tofu with cranberries, Jesus Christ, dandelion leaves sautéed with mint jelly, garlic, and olive oil, Jesus Christ, brains, eggs, and pumpkin casserole, Jesus Christ, odd but enthralling, right, *Isolate Flecks* is published, Vance Whitestone, right, reviews it, he's, well, somewhat unkind, you know, a little harsh, right, he doesn't much care, you know, for the book, he, well, actually he crucifies it, too bad, Leo cries, he cries a lot lately, Ellen's pink dress doesn't help, she won't do what Leo likes anymore, she stops buying refill paper for his leather notebooks, she's, you know, got other fish, you know, to fry, she moves out one day, temporarily, to stay with Roberte, just for a few, right, a few, a short, right, some weeks, time flies, a month or two, she moves her clothes in, her record player, her books, Roberte is writing the text, the commentary, you know, for *Annals of Sapphism: Womanlove*, and one thing, you know, one thing just sort of leads to another, Roberte shows Ellen certain things, certain, you know, techniques, right, Ellen meets Lucy Taylor, someone who is, well, Lucy is in love with Joanne Lewis, because Joanne is, well, Joanne is really lovely, and besides, her so-called husband, Guy, the so-called artist, right, he's up to his ears in something with that guy, what's his name, the twisted creepy guy, with the bum leg, no, with the limp, no, the guy with the clubfoot, with that horrible blue suit, oh God, and Guy gives beautiful Joanne no peace, so Joanne and Lucy, after all, what the hell, Ellen and Lucy hit it off, they begin to live together, Leo is out in the cold, too bad, Ellen and Anne have a long talk together one night at The Black Basement, a new club that Jackie has just opened up, no, that Jackie manages, they find, you know, that they have a lot to, well, to talk about, right, they agree that Leo is, well, you know, that Leo is, well, Jesus Christ, they become friends, they talk things over, one day Ellen sees Leo on the street, they call him, you know, the bard, right, she and Anne, Ellen sees the bard on the street, pathetic, unshaven, under his arm he has this copy of, right, *Isolate Flecks,* pitiful, too bad, he doesn't, you know, recognize her, he can't recognize her, even though he looks, Jesus Christ, he looks right in her face, her new look, her crew cut, her, you know, her new self, overalls, fedora, right, the same fedora that, right, work boots, she smiles at Roberte, who is with her, they go into the Caliph's Walk, she has to call Jackie, she has to make, you know, arrangement, to get, well, to get the plans straight for the High Holidays, for Passover, the seder, then she has to go and buy a wig, you know, and a nice little black dress, right, because, you know, Jack and Jackie, well, and when she comes out of the bar with Roberte, Leo is sitting on the curb, pathetic, he's drooling, he's wet his pants, Jesus Christ, disgusting, too, you know, too bad, and time flies.

Two mose bankes

Madame Annette Lorpailleur

Annette was born in Mexico of Hungarian parents who were fleeing freedom or something reasonably identical with it. How the mariachis burned the tongue, was it not so? Yet she, rather too obviously, grew up on the outskirts of London, where the depressing albeit picturesque fogs instilled in her a love for oranges, so that even today she likes to be surrounded by them in the odd moments she snatches from her busy life, well, perhaps not literally *surrounded.* She read many books, classics all, painted with a gracious nod at insouciance, and was soon married to a man who would later be disgraced, poor sweet bumbling Tommy! Something to do with bribery in the construction business. Yet none of these travails, whose enumeration is tedious but absolutely necessary to our narrative, prevented her from a relentless and single-minded pursuit of her goals, ever receding, a pursuit occasionally inter-rupted by reckless and malicious charges brought against her person, always in whispers, by the rest of the faculty. Few had number two pencils either, yet nothing seemed able to stop them.

Yes, she had found a home at last. Gone the long nights of seedy sexual adventure, the torn half-slips, the picnics and wienie roasts on the banks of the sullen and brooding Thames. Degradation is too mild a word! She knew that she looked good, even fetching, in her severe tweeds and flannels, chastely cut, sure, yet alluringly contrasted with her strong and beautifully molded legs, encased, in the time-honored phrase of Wordsworth, "in nylons taut like gold to fairy thinness beat." Talk about poetry! The flirtations with shadowy Hindu "blood cults" did not in the least prevent her from pottering in her garden, a formal English garden, as one might expect, in the elegantly restrained village of Stilton-on-Baskerville, where the lawns had been sown at the time of

William the Conqueror's birth. His royal mother, so the story goes, had asked for preserves of some kind as she expired. Noblesse oblige! Often the young Annette gamboled, Heidegger all forgotten, in nothing but the bottom part, or the "pants," of a swimsuit casually selected and purchased in Rio. Lord Harlan wasn't quite sure whether he liked that, and would sometimes glance up from his blueprints disapprovingly. Yet at dinner at the Macedero Club that evening, or the Blue Rune, or Le Bricoleur, when Madame's hand stole softly beneath the immaculate napery and rested, rather promisingly, it must be added, on his trouser-fly, he would find himself ordering in his most compelling, though somewhat theatrical, tone of voice. And *what* he ordered! Even the *maître d'hôtel* averted his experienced eyes.

Often a tree would fall as she labored over her footnotes. Then would follow a lengthy discussion of love and the responsibilities attendant thereon. Sleep was, of course, difficult. But nothing could keep her from the meal that she loved to prepare in the mornings for her Tommy. She also "fell to," as Stevenson might say, with a hearty appetite. And coffee? Well! Long into the mornings, graceful in her flowery peignoir, she sipped at the brew, her thoughts far away, the house quiet, Tommy at one of his many offices, or, as he'd often whispered to her, his "branches." His voice, at such times, had that edge of gruffness to it that was sure to soften her heart and permit her to forgive him, even though the ancestral English oak had, yet again, smashed in the roof. At such times Zeno helped, as did Cleanthes of Assos, and, goodness knows, it was wonderful old Chrysippus of Soli who had enabled her to cope with the discovery that somebody, probably the sturdy gardener, had allowed a bushel of corn to rot in the hold of the yacht, the older one, thank goodness!

After Tommy had been slandered and hounded by a vengeful and vulgar press to his exile in one of the larger Midwestern states, where even now he regales the members of the Country Club with bantering descriptions of scones, Annette (or, as she still bravely and defiantly calls herself on those rare occasions when she puts pen to paper to thank an old friend, and how few of them were left!, for a gift of marmalade or a dead turkey, perhaps a potted boar's head—Lady Granjon *still* knew what she liked!—Lady Harlan), Annette, ever in command, had turned her hand to the composition of "spicy" limericks, many of which she threw wildly into the sea. There was something disconcerting about them, or so she admitted to a bevy of chuckling journalists. One of them snagged her revealing skirt on the quince, and *who* shouldered the blame? Of course!

Still, the reviews were wonderful, so much so that her colleagues often gave a party or two, anything, as they said, but not to Annette, whom they still hated, to get a "celeb" onto the hoary, yet not unattractive grounds of the university. Many would gather beneath the statue, as if *that* would help. These academics! That she chose, at this time, to dispense with underclothing, is apparent in the dust-jacket photograph, which shows her, somewhat bemused, before a wall of books in her study. A discerning eye can descry some several oak branches protruding from the ceiling. Yet *nobody,* not even the Earl of Bodoni or Tony Malinger, fresh from yet another triumph at Cannes, was permitted to smoke. She had, it was obvious, heard a few things. Instead, they spoke of the great satisfaction her garden gave them, as well as the ineffable peace they found, pink gins in hand, in the bee-loud maid. There were, of needs, a few guests who were quite painfully stung by the irrepressible forest creatures, but Reeve, the head butler, always had to hand plenty of lard and seasoned chaff. Good old Reeve! His collection of curious implements was a "hit" with the Frankenstein girls, the minxes! And still the reviews came in!, one, as her publisher, Freddie Willingmouth, put it, better than the other. There was, as Lady Harlan told Mrs. Divan of the Condom League, something "about" Freddie. Others of their set agreed, but rarely.

At the Academy Awards ceremony, no one, it seemed, in all that glittering assemblage of wealth and talent, was surprised when *Fly of Metal* won virtually every award. When Annette kissed her "Oscar" and spoke, quite movingly, of her old dining table, wittily characterized by her as a "groaning board," even the little people got to their feet. They were something that night! Later, at the whirl of parties, the President called and gave her a lighthearted description of his Windsor knot. And people wonder why! Still, she would have thought it odd, if not remarkable, had she known that the strange odor in her dressing room was caused by a moldering copy of the *Tractatus,* left there, in hasty retreat, by an old school chum, Berthe Delamode, who, as Corrie Corriendo, presided over one of the more exclusive brothels in all of

Beverly Hills, though the envious scoffed. Let them! others proclaimed. How Annette herself had fought her feelings when she found Berthe's fondly inscribed packet of pornographic playing cards. Had our country's enemies ever got their hands on the Five of Clubs! Heavens! Yet she triumphed over her animal emotions, as was her wont. Berthe's fedora, however, was found the next morning by the chambermaid, submerged and as good as ruined in the loo. Curious word! Tommy read, some weeks later, and with no small degree of hilarity, of the team of plumbers and their search for an orange, "caught," as the manager put it, "somewhere in the miles of pipes" beneath the hotel. Poor Berthe! Yet the nagging realization that Annette had once owned a fedora caused him, no longer as young as he had once been, many a sleepless night. Slipping into the "frillies" that his fiancée had bought for him at François of Fargo's gave him, thank goodness, some surcease from the pain of suspicion. And one night, what should appear on the "telly" in his suite but an old Jeff Chandler "flick"! There had always been something infectious about *that* he-man, so the gossip went. Society columnists were increasingly grumbling, however, that the season was not quite the same as it had been when he'd brusquely organized generally amusing orgies, a few of which had been of a decidedly sexual bent. Yet on Thursday evenings, lost in nostalgia, he would stare at her photograph and remember. Still, nothing could deny that the frame cried out to be replaced. One morning, he flew into a rage when his favorite magazine lacked an ad that reliably confused him. It looked like "the end of the line," as Dreiser once wrote to an old friend who still, after all these years, lives in Tucson with her memories.

In any case, the money, which Professor Blinque facetiously characterized as "moolah," rolled in. What a card! She was in time given an endowed chair, and then it was that the wives of her colleagues no longer asked what she "did." But nothing, it seemed, could help. Soon, fellatio itself was a bust and the mullioned window, although repaired, lacked the old zing. She wanted, most desperately, to be believable, despite her odd proclivities for public self-abuse, or "pollution," as Father Debris liked to call it. Oh, she *read* everything! But many the night found her dreamily washing the ashtray her cousin, Welles, had made, for a lark, at Cambridge. Remarkable how after the Sudan we have tended to forgive fraternity boys everything. The Museum of

Modern Art in New York was interested but cautious. They'd had *their* share! It was less of a shock than a surprise when the headlines screamed of Welles's disappearance in the Amazon Basin. They *had* found a pith helmet sporting nine poisoned darts. Cold comfort indeed. Never again would the flaxen-haired youth lurk in the men's rooms of the bustling Métro! Nevertheless, the old English oak appeared to be growing again. And then Berthe was heard from, as if out of the blue. How could she have dreamed *that?* Yet records indicate, if one reads between the lines, that it was so. From that soft afternoon to her first pair of metal shoes was the simplest of progressions, so that even Baron Sternhagen was compelled to extinguish his cheroot before attempting his sexual specialty, no small victory! Lady Harlan wasn't through yet, despite an irritable deluge of the new season's great novels. Hadn't the Dean of Arts and Sciences given her a new nameplate for her door? No matter that her name was spelled "Onette." That had *always* been a minor flaw. There was always the potato salad and the chance to filch a seasoned cardigan while everyone took snapshots of the much-heralded event. The paperback was doing well, too, and though Tommy had taken to sending her descriptions and photographs of his new family, the elms had, for *once,* escaped.

The metal slips were somewhat of a bother, but Annette remembered Edison and his onanistic interludes, and Berthe only laughed. It was the same dry, hard, brittle, forced laugh that had made her so loathed at Greengage School. Lady Harlan had, in spite of it all, become something of a "looker," though diet and exercise had taken their toll. Still, tongues wagged. Hadn't Charles Rimini-Bates returned the garter, the "something blue," he'd stolen after that weekend in the Newlywed Room? Annette felt a *little* sorry for herself, but decided definitely against the chain-mail. Enough was enough! Later, when the apartment had somehow dissolved, there would be time for a nostalgic tear or two. In the meantime there were the term papers, the Committee Against the Committee on Committees, the domestic wines—quite good in their way—and new studies of the Bloomsbury circle, though few understood her dogged insistence that Jack London had actually written *The Voyage Out.* Indeed, there were some who demanded that she "go back to Hollywood." No amount of sparkling water could placate *them.* She thought, one bright, crisp autumn day, relaxing on a flat rock in the middle of a New England field, of the old English oak, but soon rejected the idea as gauche. It was, indeed, for many of her younger colleagues, a pleasure to get to know her. Although her skirts were becoming disconcertingly short—the New York influence, some opined—few, if any, left early. Then, too, there were the long nights of Key Lime pies, the slide shows, just about any kind of World War I model plane, and, for a lucky few, oral sex with unknown but complaisant guests in the potting shed. How they treasured their inscribed copies! No one knew, of course, that Tommy had taken up a stubborn yet fitful residence in the attic. Marmalade was, Annette was chagrined to admit, but his second choice. It is difficult to understand the creative spirit. Berthe, at any rate, finally decided she wanted him in her employ, for the "few old broads," as she facetiously put it, who'd arrive after midnight. There was the usual rouge and the occasional blushing remonstration, but nothing could stop Tommy once he had his trousers off. Dear Berthe! Lady Harlan's next book, the memoirs, wasn't half-bad, so everyone said. But she did get some odd looks on the old quad. Luckily, she had her chair, and the rights had been bought for an Academic Playhouse of the Air dramatization. She even found herself chatting with her colleagues and their auto mechanics as the cool of the evening descended on the trees. Strange how often they spoke of Europe. When the wind blew up, the trees soughed, and the gossip turned to marital problems, which, the "gang" agreed, were a bother. Still, *somebody* had to open the summer cottage.

Then there were the reflecting floors, the rare-book collection, the evenings spent sorting out her blouses and the few intimate garments, which she, in high spirits, called "lingerie," and which she couldn't bear to pass on to the maid. It was, in truth, absurd to find that on numerous occasions, a man who introduced himself as Mr. Rosette was discovered cowering behind a rack of evening gowns. He looked older than usual, but what, in heaven's name, was she expected to do about that? Nor was it her fault if Sheila, who had often loudly proclaimed her friendship, insisted on cavorting, as good as naked, in the street. She'd always maliciously called her Lady *Harley* anyway. Tommy, as usual, wasn't talking, poor darling. Yet the blame, if blame it was, had to be placed somewhere. Surely, Annette hadn't intended on actually *working* in the bordello. It had been merely a misunderstanding that "caught her out" entertaining two priests, a policewoman, and someone who kept insisting, over and over, that he was "lost." The subsequent faculty meeting was lively, to say the least. It seems that no one dared venture to put in a good word for either Virginia *or* Leonard Woolf. On the contrary, one distinguished professor, in the slow and measured tones of an engaging pedantry, suggested that they were, after all, "only British," and, as such, decidedly vulgar. There ensued a confused rush to the coffee machine.

But by this time the yacht had been refitted despite all, and Bermuda was, Annette wrote to a favored few, beautiful for a change, even though Tommy kept insisting, long-distance, that he had married Karen in a moment of pique. One can't have everything. So it wasn't with precisely a *light* heart that Lady Harlan threw everything over and boarded her favorite luxury liner with her "little Hungarian," Count Janos something-or-other. Pity his mother had ordered his tubes tied after the Cracow affair with a band of traveling goodwill ambassadors. Still, her collection of Impressionists was dazzling, if banal. The university, however, never quite recovered from the blow, nor did it go unnoticed that three new female assistant professors had taken to affecting tweed suits and low-heeled shoes. Though they often tried surreptitiously to cover their knees at faculty "galas," many old hands were having none of *that,* thank you! There was *always* too much to drink. And so it was that a daughter was born at last. The Count looked on amazed for the space of a few moments, then fled to his estate. Annette, or as she was now called by her ideologically naive new friends, Countess Nettie, ate another forbidden chocolate. There was little to be done about it, for now the *shrubs* seemed to be toppling over, some of them onto the greenhouse. That spelled disaster, of course, for an awful lot of flowers. But it would be champagne and caviar for everyone sometime soon, even tough-guy writers. How the moonlight danced on the waves, and that glow in the distance was surely Miami! So life, Nettie mused, smiling gently into the refreshing salt spray, did have a meaning after all. More or less.

Ann Taylor Redding

Although there were a few Bulgarian friends left in Panama when Dr.

Redding decided to leave, she wasn't that impressed. "The grass *is* always greener," she'd quip, packing her favorite stocks and foulards. And she never wanted to see goulash again! No one dared ask why, amid the general hubbub beneath her window. Had they surmised that her favorite leather bag was crammed with peaches and apricots, they might have changed their tune, although certain highly placed commentators still deride that idea. Yet Paris was, as always, Paris. There it lay! Ann knew that she could always count on a good, depressing drizzle to make her forget the banana plantations and the other things, mostly multicolored. Still, a therapeutic bout of blubbering and wailing insured the presence, sometimes for days, of what she had learned to call a "cafard." Those frogs!, she spasmodically tittered through her sobs. And although she had never married, she couldn't forget her new business associate, Mr. Pungoe. He wore his electric-blue suit everywhere, while the other partners sat and grumbled in New York and other humming capitals. A few said it was the real-estate dodge that drove them into their weekly frenzies. Yet the majority was closer to the truth. On the other hand it took no great acumen to search out the real factors behind it all. Ann was back and show business was once more beginning to pick up, a sure sign that the party season was upon them. We *think* we know what cocktails are! And platters with unrecognizable cheeses! So the good doctor was, take it all in all, glad to be "home" again, faced, though she was, with her world-renowned sportswear collection. *Somebody* had to do it.

She'd gaze out at the Loire, the Eiffel Tower throwing its brooding shadow on her biscuit. Then, of a sudden, there were the stars! What with her recipes, various engines of destruction, her silks and satins, the shoes that *still* didn't fit, and the few, poor, steel brassieres she'd made —how many years ago was it now?—in Indochina, the nights would pass. She didn't mind a bit! Every other Tuesday would, however, find her on the window ledge, the subject of prying eyes, but the famous lines, "Something there is that doesn't love a fall," kept her from it. That's art for you! Friends? Well, perhaps, but it wasn't always so. But with the mere act of kindling a good fire, and placing a white cloth on the table, things often began to "look up." With wheat rolls and a glass of fresh clear water, Ann managed to engineer a *few* pleasures for herself. "Besticitum consolatio veni ad me vertat Creon, Creon, Creon," she'd begin one. Then, look out! By the time the newspapers got wind of the various occurrences, Dr. Redding had lit out for her château at Après-le-Bain. It was whispered by the grooms and a few others that Richelieu himself had breakfasted on rotten *oeufs* in the homely kitchen. Wittgenstein *was* a comfort, even though her habit of reading him in the chimney corner in a swimsuit set the surrounding countryside abuzz. Soon after, the mad garageman escaped and the cows, so it was bruited about, ran for their very lives! That very week, the Board of Directors voted to ask for her resignation. What a joke! She'd occasionally call long-distance and talk, in that odd voice of hers, to just about *anybody.* Pungoe, just in from his morning tramp—an old war "buddy" who had fallen on hard times—didn't precisely *object,* yet there was something in his face that gave her pause. All would be forgotten in the evenings, however, when, at Club Zappe, or the Hotel Pachuco, or Le Bleu du Ciel, Ann's shining gauntlet paddled in the entrée in such wise as to make Pungoe literally *drag* her home. And so to bed! *That's* where his clubfoot came in handy. But in the mornings the shrubs were dying. Oh, she'd turn to her ledgers and account books, of course, but even Ann couldn't blot out the fact that her diploma was, well, *missing.* Pungoe, dear heart, jovially spoke of the letters to the advice columnists, and poured the wine with a liberal hand. Still and all. And the *meals,* especially dinner! But back in her room, Ann waited tensely for the door to slam. Connecticut again?, she'd often think, then vomit, like as not. Pungoe had become, willy-nilly, a man on the go. And she, somewhat tragically, had tired of the endless hors d'oeuvres and a couple of cherished memories. Perhaps it was polishing her evening gowns that kept her sane. Still, there were *other* stories. Beauchamp, the hostler, was found one morning caught fast in the trellis. A stern look from Ann put a stop, eventually, to *that.*

Meanwhile, somewhere in the middle of the great city, Pungoe had become involved in "the arts," whatever in the world he meant by that. The notorious Horace Rosette, "the man without a patio," as he was known to the seething milieu, was behind him, a remark that occasioned many a furtive leer. Little, if any, decency was shown. Ann rummaged through the fallen leaves, searching for something, something. Perhaps the glove that dared not speak its name? Who could tell? But old friends from the "Zone" were always near to prevent her from savaging the phlox. You'd never have guessed, of course! "Reticent" is perhaps the word. When the reporters, who were indefatigable, scaled the wall, Countess O'Mara, Lady Bustier, and "Queen" Endiva opened fire on the ptarmigans, the loves! Even though her royalties on the first five-thousand copies of her "confessions," *A Bed of Poses*, were earmarked for the National Multiple Orgasm Fund, the stories came out twisted, as usual, in the tabloids. Partners fumed behind locked doors. They hadn't counted on *that!* Although Pungoe's complaints fell on deaf ears, Dr. Redding *would* give the party. But the hashish did its job, despite the tendency of a few high-powered executives to fall into the pool. And besides, as Lady Bustier chuckled, the videotapes of perverted Congresspersons would come in handy, later, when they found themselves touching down at Palm Springs. None were prepared, however, to discover that the top model was one of our crustiest generals. There's *something* about a soldier, one wag at the bar noted, to general acclaim.

So went the weekends. The maids quit, *en masse*, every Monday morning. "Incidents," one petition stipulated. The Frankenstein sisters, who were usually found plodding down the sylvan back roads, loved to "fill in," however. The critical attacks on *Bed*, led by Michelle Caccatanto, were somewhat tempered by their frilly aprons and unfailing good humor. And talk about your pasta! Suffice it to say that there wasn't a tablespoon to be found. Few wanted *really* to do it, what with the children just next door, but even religion has to take a holiday *sometimes*. Hollywood was naturally interested after the talk shows, particularly the one on which Ann talked for almost ten minutes about her steel-mesh stockings. The audience roared its approval. And quips? Don't ask! But where in goodness' name were the actors? Oh, they did find a few practicing their salutes and speeches, but the moguls were, well, not happy. The option later arrived by registered mail, but it was all done so *subtly*. Pungoe had wired that Annie Flammard was more than interested but was having a spot of trouble with motivation. Still. And on top of all that, the peaches and apricots rotted, then *attacked*. It was enough to make a girl cry, or so Ann was quoted as saying. Almost immediately after, a piece by the President of the Tribade Conspiracie appeared on the op-ed pages of several major newspapers. Then, of course, came the veritable *storm* of fedoras.

Pungoe, as restless as ever, had put Rosette in his place, and an invitation quickly arrived for Dr. Redding to attend the cocktail party celebrating the opening of his new boutique, Nuts & Bolts. She literally *flew* to the wardrobe to find, as she had feared, her unique prototype for an aluminum-alloy sun dress missing. So he *had* finally decided to pattern his lackadaisical existence on the base character of Minna von Hattiesburg. What film buff worth the name doesn't recall her as she was played by Dolores Délire in *From Natchez to Mobile*? Some suggest that popcorn rose to prominence about that time. *That* was an era! Still, it is only in dusty and forgotten tomes that the role of the Iowa Writers' Workshop can be discerned in the affair. In brief, at a certain point, all admitted to a general collapse, then, in a past Director's phrase, all hell busted loose! Literary historians agree that the debacle was caused by "the short story." A few have been preserved as cautionary devices at which the curious gape with a mixture of horror and loathing. Oddly enough, children seem to like them. Ann often reflected on all this as she signed things. Pungoe *was* persistent, the boutique was flourishing, and prayer had returned. With, so to speak, a bang! Yet Dr. Redding's bank statements told the harsh truth. Cash had ceased to flow! Through the long winter, she stared unseeingly at the shriveled carrots. There was, surely, her platinum cocktail-dress collection, safe in Marrakesh. But then her father's gruff voice and work-gnarled hands would come back to haunt her dreams. Annie Flammard? Ann would wake up, once in a while, in a cold sweat.

It was at about that time, at the advice of her psychoanalyst, Miriam Paimon, that she decided to "act out"; in the words of Dr. Paimon, "What the fuck." Good advice indeed, as it turned out. Ann journeyed to the Everglades and started what is still spoken of with awe in the real-estate business as one fantastic scam. An adroit mixture of senior citizens, condominiums, and faulty building materials, and in no time at all she was giving speeches and winning awards. Money? It is to laugh. But in a trice, her sister died, found smothered beneath a pile of *Cosmopolitans* and *Swedish Lusts* in a sordid room of the New Ecstasy Motor Inn. A few Evangelists spoke of sin and free school lunches, but they buried her anyway. An old friend, Karen, called during the funeral festivities, to let Ann know that all had turned out badly. She *had* managed to marry Lord Ridingcrop, whom she somewhat unfairly referred to as "an English pipsqueak." Street toughs had long known where to sell their "hot" garter belts, but still, Ridie had a few good points. For one, he *was* British, or so the *Times* had long assumed. Subsequently, there was that indefinable *soupçon* of elegance, of grace, about him. Perhaps it was his kippers! Certainly, no one else in Riding-on-Alum wore them with such an easy flair. Unfortunately, when he rode to hounds, the young ladies hid their eyes and the older ones blushed demurely. Sports often bring odd things out.

So bad news followed on the heels of bad news, often without surcease. Ann began smoking extremely large cigars, wondering—occasionally aloud—if this nasty habit had anything to do with phallic symbols or whatever they're called. She was never one to fret, however, no matter the damned Sunday supplements. Then came the certain hearty tycoon's call! It was time to modernize her kitchen! Dr. Redding set to with a will, hammers flying, gouges and adzes and Stillson wrenches not far behind. Acclaim for the finished job was not so great as she had hoped or expected. Old friends fell silent when she entered the room and Holt Rinehart, her new maid, kept tossing his little lace caps into the garbage-disposal unit; it *was* in the sink, but unmarried young women often found themselves unwilling observers. Ann, in what Pungoe diffidently called "a tizzy," took out the fuses, but Holt had other methods up his puffy sleeve. What a rascal he was! Ann wouldn't have cared, for herself, but she'd read too many accounts of honeymoons that just weren't *fun* to let him have his way. So when the auctioneer disposed of the last Warhol—and passing acquaintances agreed that it was *amusing,* at least—the doctor took a room in a new "in" whorehouse. She had sworn to read, straight through, all the Pulitzer Prize novels of the last quarter-century. "For penance," she implored anyone who would listen. Of course, they were busy most of the time, and even she was constantly being urged by clients, who'd mostly had a few, to disrobe, at least partially. Still, on she read, with, it must be confessed, a pencil in hand. You can't *tell* about people.

A long, rambling letter arrived and in it she learned that the mesquite had just up and quit. Things were back to normal at the new ranch! She'd gaze out, thinking, *knowing* that it was too good to be true. Pungoe was discovered in the game room, morose as usual. Money, money, money! But the long winter nights were perfect for their addled and unreasonably wayward conversations, the delicious—and little known—mustards from every corner of the earth, and the semi-weekly shot at fornication in front of the crackling wassail bowl. Christmas at last! Partners, moguls, tycoons, and assorted alcoholics turned up on the doorstep, proving, if proof were needed, that they were no slouches when it came to opera and other refined, if silly, things. And double-breasted suits were back! She realized just how *long* she'd been away as she flailed wildly at a piñata. She knew, at long last, the truth of the old saying, "ethnics are warm and *real.*" You bet! she chirruped gaily.

But almost before the eggnog had turned a frightful green, it was spring! Then came the requests from adoring fans and goodness knows what all else! Skyscraper heels, surely. Pungoe adored to watch her totter about the yard at her chores, and growled happily. If marriage could only be like *this,* Ann would carelessly think in her little room under the eaves. Yet Karen was ill! One can imagine the doctor's surprise when the photographs arrived, *air mail,* from Worcestershire. As if *she* could have helped. Pungoe, as usual in times of crisis, was doing something with the chickens. Foul birds! A book she'd once read came back to her, but she wasn't going to *tell* anybody about it. Especially Ridie! She had to hold most of them upside down or side-ways to discover just *what* was going on. Medical personnel had often proved that that many people couldn't be in one place at the same time without *something* breaking. You never know with demented gay persons, so Ann claimed. There were a few loud Christian cheers, but for the most part, the desert brooded in silence. There occurred an occasional cloud of dust on the horizon, but nobody cared about *that.* Well, it wasn't their responsibility. Still, a few days later, she bought a great deal of flat-white exterior but tearfully admitted that her heart wasn't in it. She even wrote to Karen at Lourdes, "Fuck the place!" Well.

After a wild and confused meeting with the board, she went ahead and put the soft-drink machine in, and, as she had long insisted would occur, her stock soared with the lowly employees, although the clerks groused, as usual, amid the bulging files. Deals, however, soon were being closed with the greatest of alacrity and dispatch and soon the area around the water cooler was virtually empty. Dr. Paimon presented her with a signed and leatherbound monograph on what she was pleased, for some reason, to call her "case." But after a score more triumphs she tired of everything, sold her shares and her skyscraper heels to Whytte-Blorenge, the ruthless fundraiser, and married, at last, a wonderful guy that she introduced to the old crowd as Rupe. Little was known about him, save that there were sexually explicit rumors having something to do with wicker baskets from Hong Kong. But love will find a way, or so Karen wrote from the cloister. Rupe did assume some airs, but with *that* nose? Why not?, the women, at least, opined. The men were, give the devil his due, chasing the underwear models around the greenhouse, now damaged almost beyond repair! Younger female partners took over the day-to-day business and once again the clank of metal was heard in the vast midtown offices. They all certainly *gleamed!* It wasn't that, but there seemed to be, among the women, great difficulties in sitting down. These kids!, wiser heads stated. For the record! Nostalgia was king, as is its wont. "Smooth," as weeklies suggested, "sailing." And how! But for others, it just hadn't panned out at all. Pungoe, for instance, was seen in an obsolete amusement park outside Wilkes-Barre, but then, silence. No one seemed to care about the three young women facing the horror of their unloved fetuses. Oh, the letters poured in to the newspapers, but they all seemed to have to do with sin and slaughter. There is no *telling* what excites some people. Ann, however, when she heard the reports, looked blank. Those who *really* knew her weren't a bit amazed. Unforgiving, perhaps. But she, her arm around Rupe, sailed on, the two of them lost in admiration on the forecastle or some other nautical equipment. Tahiti!, she laughed into the wind! Here we come!, the crew later swore she screamed. Rupe, however, wasn't so sure, although even *he* had heard about the depraved women thereabouts, well, perhaps not actually *depraved,* but there seemed to be nothing that they couldn't be talked into. At least so said old salts. And tars. There was nothing to lose, in any event, and he expressed this opinion to his bride. Ann threw him a fond but prurient glance as the pole star twinkled. It seemed to suggest that life was for living.

Tree of gowlden apples

Bart Kahane, who you will certainly remember may have been seriously injured some twenty or twenty-five years ago as the direct result of his penchant for donning women's clothing, or so we have been led to believe, decided, when he first married Conchita, which was a pet name for her true name, María de la Concepción, full name, María de la Concepción Dorotea Carolina Darío y Reyes, to find out all that he could about her seven sisters. His reasons for doing this are best known to Bart, who seems to be in a coma, and to his mother, who has disappeared. These seven sisters had all married suitable husbands, according, that is, to Conchita, the "flower of Durango," or, as she sometimes called herself, the "flower de Durango." Whenever Bart thought, when he could think, of this group of fourteen, or sixteen, if he added, as he invariably did, Conchita and himself, he visualized a small tree, perfectly spherical in the shape of its leafy branches, and dotted here and there with apples—golden apples. A rather too obvious figure, it is true, but one suitable to Bart's poetic understanding. Let us say immediately that he had a penchant for what is often called "the image." It is not too much to say also that this by-now famous "tree" and its equally famous "golden apples" have been made part of the accoutrements of Bart's "mind" because of the title of this section. The secrets of art are long, long secrets.

There were, in addition to lovely Conchita, lissome Constanza, beauteous Berta, gorgeous Elisa, handsome Eugenia, plain Lucía, sultry Bárbara, and vivacious Benita. A bevy of hot tamales, as Bart often put it to his many friends and acquaintances, whose identities are, let us hope, well known by now. The tamales' natural desires for home, security, and children, coupled with their fiancés' impetuous lusts, made for a series of quick marriages, beginning with that of the lovely Conchita to the twisted Bart. Then, in rapid succession, or, as Bart would sometimes humorously say, *pronto,* the lissome Constanza married the wily Charles "Chuck" Murphy, the beauteous Berta the good-natured Albert "Hap" Garrett, the gorgeous Elisa the saturnine Louis "Slim" Hess, the handsome Eugenia the effeminate William "LuLu" Hunter, the plain Lucía the ugly Henry "Hank" Lewison, the sultry Bárbara the lecherous Al "Whitey" Shields, and the vivacious Benita the pious Charles "Chick" O'Hearn. Strange, as the phrase has it, bedfellows, although more than one of the deliriously joyful newlyweds had never heard this expression. Hence the occasional grunt of bewilderment or chagrin when these particular unfortunates ran across the term in their honeymoon reading. For all, or most of them, had taken a good supply of books and periodicals into their various nuptial chambers.

The eight women, seized by the female aberration known to medicine as "the vapors" [See Lange, *Traité des vapeurs* (Paris, 1689); Raulin, *Traité des affections vaporeuses du sexe* (Paris, 1758); Pressavin, *Nouveau Traité des vapeurs* (Lyons, 1770); Rostaing, *Réflexions sur les affections vaporeuses* (Paris, 1778)], decided, in concert, to call their husbands by nicknames to which only the sisters would be privy. Thus, Bart was to be known as "Nando," Charles "Chuck" as "Carlos," Albert "Hap" as "Paco," Louis "Slim" as "Che," William "LuLu" as "Rosita," Henry "Hank" as "Chico," Al "Whitey" as "Pablito," and Charles "Chick" as "Momo." The root causes for this collective gesture toward sisterly unity are unknown despite our admittedly careless and halfhearted attempts at research, although a few amateurs who have concerned themselves with this mildly surprising but not unprecedented act seem to agree that a working premise, or opinion, may be based on the invaluable though somewhat eccentric studies of the "naming malady" done by "the man who ate the broom," Edmé-Pierre Beauchesne in his often-mocked *De l'influence des affections de l'âme dans les maladies nerveuses des femmes* (Paris, 1783). That work has since been, of course, superseded by the clinical observations of Pearson, Kooba, Beshary, *et al.,* yet its implications are, to this day, suggestive.

Perhaps more interestingly, the eight husbands, acting, for the nonce, in ignorance of their wives' decision, decided to take unto themselves nicknames as well, in order, as one of them later admitted, to feel closer

. . . to each other. So that Bart "Nando" was to be known as "Beebee," Charles "Chuck" "Carlos" as "Chaz," Albert "Hap" "Paco" as "Allie," Louis "Slim" "Che" as "Luigi," William "Lulu" "Rosita" as "Sweetums," Henry "Hank" "Chico" as "Hen," Al "Whitey" "Pablito" as "Happy," and Charles "Chick" "Momo" as "Cheech."

Bart, whose well-known oddities of behavior go far in explaining the obsessive interest he took in the activities of his in-laws, may have initially conceived of the eight marriages as a vast *hieros gamos.* If so, it was the very holiness of the rite which was to afford him, paradoxically, the greatest amusement, in that the second year of marriage for each couple revealed that all of the partners had availed themselves of lovers. For the sake of what we must insistently call the record, these pairings were: Conchita Kahane and Keith Blague; Constanza Murphy and Edmund Posherde; Berta Garrett and Emmanuel Chanko; Elisa Hess and Joe Billy Tupelo; Eugenia Hunter and Chalmers Endicott-Braxton; Lucía Lewison and "Weeps" McGuire; Bárbara Shields and Jay Bindle; Benita O'Hearn and "Buddy" Cioppetini; Bart "Nando" "Beebee" Kahane and Lolita Schiller; Charles "Chuck" "Carlos" "Chaz" Murphy and "Chickie" Levine; Albert "Hap" "Paco" "Allie" Garrett and Diane Drought; Louis "Slim" "Che" "Luigi" Hess and "Tits" O'Rourke; William "Lulu" "Rosita" "Sweetums" Hunter and "Buzz" Duncan; Henry "Hank" "Chico" "Hen" Lewison and "Muffin" Cunningham; Al "Whitey" "Pablito" "Happy" Shields and Eleanor Julienne; and Charles "Chick" "Momo" "Cheech" O'Hearn and Marie Louise Wong.

Now, according to hastily scraped-together information, Bart, in those few lucid intervals that interrupt his coma, as golden apples interrupt the green field of the tree from which they depend, hysterically insists that the eight sisters found each other's lovers to be far more interesting and desirable than the individuals whom each had originally seduced, or been seduced by. So that each, if Bart's ramblings are to be believed, began a clandestine affair with a fresh partner. In order to conceal, as best they could, their liaisons from each other, from their primary lovers, and, of course, from their husbands, assuming that their husbands, in the throes of their own amorous passions, cared about either their primary or secondary lovers, each took unto herself a name to be used while engaged in her secret venery, and also gave unto her new lover a secret name. Thus, Conchita Kahane as "Babs" or "Boobs" Gonzales or Consundays took up with Edmund Posherde, whom she called "Blinky" or "Bunky"; Constanza Murphy as "Queenie" or "Cunty" Antilles or Uncles with Emmanuel Chanko, whom she called "Puppo" or "Peepee"; Berta Garrett as "Honey" or "Hummy" Potts or Pazzo with Joe Billy Tupelo, whom she called "Texie" or "Taxi"; Elisa Hess as "Giggles" or "Gallie" Whinge or Bilge with Chalmers Endicott-Braxton, whom she called "Paleface" or "Polefast"; Eugenia Hunter as "Big Mama" or "Bag Mama" Pussie or Fussy with "Weeps" McGuire, whom she called "Fotz" or "Fudge"; Lucía Lewison as "Jitters" or "Cheesy" Staffel or Stuffit with Jay Bindle, whom she called "Heeb" or "Hoib"; Bárbara Shields as "Hots" or "Humps" Reilly or Daly with "Buddy" Cioppetini, whom she called "Hoagie" or "Doggie"; and Benita O'Hearn as "Legs" or "Sucks" Tubetti or Tortoni with Keith Blague, whom she called "Joker" or "Joan."

On, so to speak, the masculine side of these marriages, the arrow of Eros was also indiscriminately striking the sisters' husbands, and they followed, as if under a spell, the sort of spell that strikes one upon first glimpsing a tree, soft in the morning mist, crowded with golden apples, their wives' leads. And, too, for purposes of concealment, they availed themselves, while engaged in their carnal pursuits, of the nicknames that their wives had earlier given them. Bart is too "loco" and we are too busy to resolve the appealing mystery of how the husbands discovered their wives' secret names for them, but the evidence, flimsy as it is, shows that discover them they did. So that Bart Kahane as "Nando" dallied with "Chickie" Levine, whom he knew as "Lips," the pet name that Charles had given her; Charles Murphy as "Carlos" with Diane Drought, whom he knew as "Hickey," the pet name that Albert had given her; Albert Garrett as "Paco" with "Tits" O'Rourke, whom he knew as "Big Tits," the pet name that Louis had given her; Louis Hess as "Che" with "Buzz" Duncan, whom he knew as "Buns," the pet name that William had given him; William Hunter as "Rosita" with "Muffin"Cunningham, whom he knew as "Scummy," the pet name that Henry had given her; Henry Lewison as "Chico" with Eleanor Julienne, whom he knew as "Taterhead," the pet name that Al had given her; Al Shields as "Pablito" with Marie Louise Wong, whom he knew as "Chinks," the pet name that Charles had given her, and Charles O'Hearn as "Momo" with Lolita Schiller, whom he knew as "Dumb Lo," the pet name that Bart had given her.

It may be inferred, at this point, that these data, some, admittedly, tainted by conjecture, suggest that "the vapors" are not only progressive, but that they may be highly and intersexually communicable.

Bart's "tree," we note, was now more full of "golden apples" than he had bargained for. His transvestite quirks may have well been, in fact, the direct result of his growing bewilderment and anxiety concerning the moral configuration of this voluptuous and shifting panorama, or, as Bart once put it, this "fucking circus." His anxiety was surely not ameliorated by the fact that another "crop" of "apples" was, over a period of some twenty years, brought into the world. These were, of course, the children born to these various couplings, lawful and otherwise. It is impossible to assign to these children their proper and/or responsible parents. The ceaseless copulations of the group of husbands, wives, and lovers, along with what must have been their unified effort to expunge, destroy, obliterate, erase, obscure, falsify, counterfeit, and efface all records pertinent to these various births, has made it difficult even to begin to trace genealogies. We must permit, so to speak, these children simply to "appear." Here follows an incomplete listing of these offspring:

Nemo, Chooch, Hoppy, YoYo, "Mutt," Hips, Jiggs, Eppie, Looy, Slug, Ignatz, "Fotch," Popeye, Blast, Walt, Krazy, "Hans," Socks, Andy, Lefty, Jeff, Whitey, Skeezix, Blue Wind, "Ben," U.P., Swee'pea, Dipers, Chester, Chet, Chatz, Bud, Slam, Terry, Holo, "Clark," Fems, Whammo, Slick, Tillie, Trixie, Bra, Blondie, Blinky, Blow, Traxy, Mille, "Dick," Blammo, Hem, "Mark," Soho, Perrie, Bam, Mud, Matz, Zet, Hester, Weepers, DeeJee, Op, "Wen," Oiwin, Mannix, Blightie, Heff, Hefty, Mandie, Cox, "Mans," Hazie, Balte, Mast, Woppie, "Scotch," Oogotz, Mugg, Duey, Zippy, Wig, Lips, "Guts," LoLo, Poppy, Scootch, and Froufrou.

Finally, it may be of value to add that at the periphery of the complex erotics herein but sketched, there were at least ninety-seven other people who had to do sexually with the noted wives, husbands, and lovers. We know, if that is the word, the names of but eleven of them: Sailor Steve, Jayzus McGlade, George the Polack III, John Greene

Czcu, Miner X. Beely, Werner Smitts, Marion Bunt, Eloise Stephanie Gump, Kate O'Sighle, Patience St. James, and Whitney fFrench-Newport. All of these people seem to have disappeared, but for Patience St. James, who reads Tarot cards and tea leaves in a small store located in a large city whose name remains unknown. Her professional identity is, variously, Ronda the Crazy Gypsy and Sweaty Patsy.

In conclusion, it may be seen that rigorous attention to the most pedestrian details of human relationships may yield surprising data if not any decent "yarns." Such data, while probably of little use to an understanding of the people involved in said relationships, may, however, allow us to draw certain conclusions about the truth behind the facade of social, public intercourse. Our paradigm is, we insist, despite the mockery we are all too used to, useful to a limited degree. Some may discern in it, perhaps, the presence of what Hans Dietrich Stöffel in his *De praestigiis amoris* (Brussels, 1884) defined as "[a] large mess (*perturbatio*) developing as if self-generated out of [a] small one."

Three tombes

Was her maiden name Ravish, Ravitch, or Banjiejicz? Was it an obviously literary act for her, at the age of six, to call her most beloved doll Lu-Lu? On what pensive occasion did she wear a flowered-print Ship 'n' Shore blouse? On what date did she decide that The Three Stooges were brilliantly surrealistic? Why was it doubtful that in moments of mild frustration she whistled "That's for Me"? Why did she wear L'Ardent perfume even though she loathed its smell? Why did she attempt suicide by putting her head into a gas-stove oven when there was easily to hand a number of potentially lethal items? Did she ever use the name Louise Ashby? On what happy occasion did she wear a pale-orange dress and a plain gold bracelet? How did the novel *La Robe orangée* change her life? Was it likely that she always wore white underwear because of a magazine article? Did she really have beautiful legs? What prompted her to insist that *The Lady in the Lake* was a modern version of *Ethan Frome*? When and why did she get a tattoo on her inner left thigh that consisted of the letters W, A, C, and O? What evidence denied the oft-repeated charge that she stole an off-white raw silk shift from the Soirée Intime? Was it true that she objected to that which she somewhat obscurely referred to as Christian pornography? Was her observation that San Francisco looked like a lot of cupcakes an original one? Did she understand Emma Bovary's anguish better than Benjamin DeMott did? Was "They Can't Take That Away from Me" her favorite song, or was this too good to be true? Why did she invariably cry when she watched *Dark Victory*? Could her heart fairly be described as aching for breaking each vow? Did she think the hot dog a bona-fide phallic symbol? Why did she think that lumpy mashed potatoes were truly American? Why did she, when speaking with academics, falsely claim that she watched only public-television programs? Why did she call a term paper she wrote for an English course "Impotence in Silver Age Poets"? Did she know that Ho Chi Minh smoked Salem cigarettes? On what bitter occasion did she say, "Fly me to the moon or at least for Christ's sake take me to the fucking zoo"? Did she intermittently fantasize herself as the Simone of *Histoire de l'Oeil?* Did Sheila's proofreading of a true-life adventure story, written for the magazine *Fist!,* contribute to her decision to become a writer? Why did she look like a whore in her modest pink jersey sleeveless dress? For what reason did she falsely claim that mauve was her favorite color? Had her name been Gert Shitzvogel, Yolanda Stuzzicadenticcio, or Myrtle Wandajajiecowicz, would her first novel, *The Orange Dress,* have received any critical attention? Was she dead?

Am I embarrassed and chagrined to discover that Lou is not the originator of the phrase, "remarks are not literature"? How many times a year do I enrage Lou by suggesting that professional football players are probably fairies? Why does Lou become angry when I tell him that I'll never read *Finnegans Wake?* Is Laguna, where Lou and I honeymooned in 1964, real, or is it, like Gstaad, an imagined place? Am I secretly annoyed when Lou uses my mascara to paint a moustache and goatee on his face? What internal evidence in Lou's poem, "Sheila Sleeping," prompts me to accuse him of writing it for and about Yvonne De Carlo? Why, when I stand before Lou in lingerie from the Soirée Intime, does he say something like "this old cat plays a lot of tenor"? Am I impressed by the tag, "a poet of small perfections," that is often hung on Lou in the contributors' notes of the little magazines in which his writings appear? Do I always close my eyes and clench my teeth when Lou undresses me? Why do Lou and I think of Prospect Park with distaste? Why don't I tell Lou the name of the friend who left a manila envelope, containing nine rather unusual photographs, in our bathroom? Why does Lou claim that he wrote the central section of *The Orange Dress?* Is the foundation-garment model whose photograph reminds Lou of me at age eighteen, me at age eighteen? What is my reaction when Lou sings "Orange-Colored Sky" just prior to saying "that was some time, baby"? Why do I become annoyed with Lou whenever we travel together on the IND? Is it possible for me to initiate divorce proceedings in Laguna? Does Lou secretly possess the manuscript of my first short fiction, "Suck my Whip"? Does Lou ever shop for me at the Soirée Intime for what he calls frillies? What are the names of the third-rate Chinese restaurants at which Lou and I dine on Monday nights? What is the nature of the telephone conversations between me and Lou when he calls me late at night from Brooklyn? How often does Lou bore me to tears by telling me of E. B. White's glorious prose style? Is it unlikely that Lou and I will make love on the floor next to the Christmas tree in my family's living room? What prompts Lou to read aloud to me from the *Psychopathology of Every-day Life*? What sexual act do Lou and I refer to when we speak of "struttin' with some barbecue"? Does Lou ever watch me engage in sexual acts with another man or other men or with another woman or other women or with another man and woman or with other men and women? Why do I poke fun at one of Lou's favorite poets, Jean Ingelow? What do I say when Lou tells me that *The Bridge* is an example of religious immanence aborted by a lack of transcendent morality? Why does Lou deny ever seeing a photograph of me, at sixteen, sitting on a flat rock in a field in Connecticut? What reasons lead me to dislike the way that Lou wears his hat, holds his knife, and sings off-key? Do I ever tell Lou what I really did in my father's sinister car, outside Nathan's Famous, in sordid Coney Island? Is there anything to the rumor that when Lou eats coffee cake he never fails to remind me of the Sunday morning on which I attempted suicide? What are my motives for telling Lou that my favorite book is *Buddy and His Boys on Mystery Mountain*? Are Lou and I alive?

Why will you call your first adulterous lover Milt, even though his name will be, remarkably, Jerrold "Jambo" Vizard? What will be the surname of "Fred," to whom you will write on December 27, 1963? Why will Thomas Thebus, of Brooklyn, New York, momentarily glimpsing you from the window of a coach in which he will be traveling from Washington to New York, think you his wife Janet? Will Delilah Crosse, the lesbian sister of whom Tania never speaks, be the chic girl with whom you will strike up a friendship at a ski resort in February 1967? How will you manage to attend the Detectives' "snow party" in Vermont without Lou's knowledge? Will you ever confess to Annie Flammard and Rose Zeppole that you'd like to play a role in a porno-graphic film? Why will you pretend to believe that the deadbeat actor whom you will permit to seduce you at Annette Lorpailleur's dinner party is, in fact, a foreign military officer? What will make you virtually certain that the anonymous author of an erotic, not to say obscene letter sent you from Flint, Michigan, is none other than Margaret McNamara Duffy, a high-school career advisor? How will it come about that your father's insistence that you be home by midnight lead directly to the loss of your virginity? Does it seem possible that on the evening that you will supposedly be killed you will make a Spam and ketchup sandwich? When you tell Ellen Kaufman that your abiding desire in life is to be a fireperson will you be poking fun at the vocation, the word, Ellen, or all three? Why will you buy a pale-blue dress of soft and filmy material when you discover that Lou is having an affair with April Detective? Will it be naïveté or malice that prompts you to discuss the character of the Tin Woodman in the presence of Annette Lorpailleur? Why will Treadcliffe Marche, a sometime male model, steal your grey fedora? What will you mean when you tell Saul Blanche that you like the homoerotic imagery in Robert Frost's poems? Is it believable that your novel, *The Orange Dress*, will be nominated for the Ralph Lauren Medal for Literature? Why, despite published claims to the contrary, will the only known photograph of you in a sylvan setting show you playing volleyball in the nude? What curious and improbable series of events will lead to your winning, along with your partner, Dave Warren, the weekly fox-trot contest at the Bluebird, a tavern near Budd Lake, New Jersey? Will it be mere coincidence that leads all your lovers to read you the Blake tercet that begins, "In a wife I would desire . . ."? Will you be justified in your embarrassment and irritation when you discover that Jack Marowitz is lying about his knowledge that Duke Washington is the alto saxophonist on the famous recording of "Ko-Ko"? What will lead you to remark to Mesdames Lorpailleur, Corriendo, and Delamode that their apartment is warm and cheery? Will your coughing fit be designed to conceal hysterical laughter or compassionate weeping when you hear Leo Kaufman read, at the Gom Gallery, his celebrated "Tit Poem Number Five"? What arcane reasons will you have for collecting every recorded version of "Clarinet Polka" that you can find? Will it be a sign of the existence and goodness of God, as Rose Zeppole maintains, that you are sterile? Will you be lying when you tell all your lovers that Lou tried to destroy your literary career in order to advance his own? Is it true that moments after Bart Kahane throws himself out a window to the street below, you will steal his sequined mauve scarf? How will it happen that in the early morning of July 12, 1971, you will find yourself deshabille in the luxurious suite of a country inn with Janos Kooba, Edward Beshary, and Albert Pearson, three men whose very existence you doubted? Will it be mere coincidence that the drawing of a woman which appears on page 113 of Conchita Kahane's copy of *Segundo Curso de Español* bears a striking resemblance to you? Why will you be chagrined to learn that Saul Blanche decided to become a homosexual for a few months, or, as he put it, "more"? What pictorial evidence will contradict your assertion that you first met Cecil Tyrell in the patio garden of Horace Rosette's apartment? What will Lou make of the fact that in Laguna, on the morning of September 11, 1964, you will greet, in the space of three-quarters of an hour, Judge Harold Wenj, Cornelius A. Ryan, Johnson Mulloon, Father Donald Debris, S.J., and Captain Craig Copro, U.S.A.F.? Why will you think of Leo Kaufman's *Isolate Flecks,* a novel his many detractors call *Leo's Lunge,* each time you eat stew? If you live, will you care about any of the above-named people, and if you die, will any of them mourn you?

Beacon

Nobody is interested in Antonia Harley although it seems to be the case that something must be said of her. No one knows why this should be the case. References, certainly, here and there, may be found, anyone can find them, curiosity, that's the main thing. They were, of course, sketchy. Little response other than a shrug or a look of what has often been described as mild interest. Very mild indeed. You know about Anton, so let's leave him out of it.

It may have value, when certain new information is posited, emendations made, corrections considered, mistakes rectified, slanders quietly erased, well, partially erased, more precisely, obscured, or twisted out of recognition, when all has been made different, then quickly forgotten. In any event, she had her place, her undeniable place, even though it was as Anton's wife. Good old Anton. References may quite easily be checked against others, and there are plenty of references and plenty of others, too many, some say. Mostly readers. But although nobody really cared, something should be said.

The procedure usual in such cases: anecdotal material, so-called.

We may find ourselves in a room. We are in a room. Small wonder that it turned out to be Antonia's room, as it is now, we thought we knew what now means and whatever else it may mean it most certainly did not mean now. Antonia's room. It had in it this, and it has in it that. It had a refrigerator and a sink and from such textual evidence you may surmise that it is a kitchen. Fill in the useless details, since we are after something more profound, something real. However, if we consider that the refrigerator, the sink, and the useless details were all evidence that this room is a kitchen, is it so because of these items or because the prose once noted them with authoritative clarity? Refrigerator. Sink. Useless details. Enough of theory.

In Antonia's kitchen the fluorescent glare ruthlessly revealed a refrigerator, a sink, and other culinary items. Everywhere, a woman's light touch is descried, e.g., a dish towel, a coffee mug filled with yellow pencils, etc. Over here this touch of care. And that one. All had that ordered look. Implements, tools. Common sense is usually best in such tense situations, that is, here we are in somebody's kitchen, hers. On the other hand, common sense may be of no help whatever. Yet it has often been discovered that in mundane items people's true selves will be revealed, so goes the pensum. However, as often as not, there is another side to it, which it was once our duty to respect. Rightly so.

It may be of some value to rummage through a drawer that was quite easily seen among the wealth of details above catalogued. There it is, right over there. Although some of the items to be discovered therein, and soon, may have belonged to Anton, that somehow was not then, nor is it now, germane to our interests. Well, here they were, or will be, and as we hoped, they indeed did make us aware of, and display, as does little else, etcetera and etcetera.

There seemed to be a stirring of interest. Our story is about to take that famous turn. On, as they say, its own.

A drawer was suddenly open. Elements, or at least fragments of Antonia's true self may surely be discovered. Stranger things have happened, but rarely in a kitchen. We know a man who liked to surprise his wife in the kitchen. One leans back in one's chair and stares reflectively at the fire. The house creaked as it settled.

The open drawer. We're getting there.

Some were beginning to show a sharp interest, while others have no doubt skipped ahead to more interesting adventures. A third group has perhaps returned to familiar tales to take what they called another crack at them. "I wonder what's in the drawer," a few said, but not in unison. Perhaps they'll be able, finally, to get the gist of the thing. Or else. One or two were people who have their troubles just like everybody else. They hang on, bravely, the little people. America. Beneath all the glitter and optimism, you never know. Some were ex-drunks whose long struggle with alcoholism has made them or will someday make them, wise. Or at least resigned. To punish us, they may give interviews concerning their courageous battles.

We've heard that it's the writer's task and we cannot argue with that. Literature has a certain redemptive quality to it, so a majority opines, and not all of them can be wholly wrong. The writer, it seems, has many tasks.

In the thick of it. All right.

Someone was currently rummaging through the drawer, albeit with gentle hands, reserved mien, with a certain respect, is not too strong a word, for the woman who was not at home, or at any rate, is not in the kitchen, or those parts of it that have been tersely described in a work-manlike and sincere prose. There is nothing that can take the place of sincerity. Craft and sincerity. Craft and sincerity and the need to, the real need to tell stories. There's been a lot of rubbish spoken of all this, but in the last analysis nothing really can take the place of one flawed human voice telling of the deepest and most important hopes and fears and weaknesses and strengths of people. Flawed people. Flawed and weak and fearful. Yet strong and hopeful. And plain. And little. Plain, little people.

Antonia may well have been somewhere else in the apartment.

Slowly, the drawer was closed. Items loom in the brooding half-light, soft as yellow flowers. There's a predicate for you. Prior to now, that was. The recently rummaging figure has become the crunch of foot-steps on the gravel driveway outside. Trees thrashed about in the cold wind, the moon sailed wildly through scattered clouds. Streaming darkly. It was a gloomy night. Many go to bed early. Open the door. He looked out the window. Crunch, went the metonymy.

A little farther and all will be made clear to you. Famous and quite familiar words, he laughed.

Yet the startling light of the kitchen showed nothing out of place. Someone had done his job well. False modesty has been thrown to the winds, and the most cynical admitted that the crucial rummaging-through-the-drawer, as it has come to be known, has produced nothing of interest but a slip of paper which has written on it what turns out to be a message, so to speak, a message whose content will prove to be uncanny. In this context. At the mention of the impending disclosure of this message, interest was piqued again, so muttered new fans, as well as some old ones, returning, however reluctantly. That such a message was discovered by chance is more than coincidence, whatever the mockery we may all, or some of us, be forced to endure. Such is the writer's task.

Yet earlier, if we have all agreed on what earlier means, or, perhaps more importantly, on what it meant, the drawer was opened, its contents rummaged through. The promised inventory was not made, yet soon all will be brought to light, but in the wrong place. Soon may as well be now.

Now is as good a time as any. Or as good a place.

Six cork coasters for party use, three bottle sealers, a package of paper cocktail napkins for party use on each of which is depicted a bleary-eyed pink elephant, a package of sewing needles of various sizes, a bay tree, a box of wooden safety matches for convivial evenings when guests drop in unexpectedly, a beer-can opener for party use, the same intrinsically loathsome, an aluminum funnel for funneling certain liquids, unprepossessing, four playing cards, six of Diamonds, four of Clubs, Ace of Diamonds, six of Diamonds, a ball of cotton twine, a yellow Princess telephone, a spool of masking tape, a crucifix purportedly blessed by the Pope with the words Hiya Your Holiness printed across its shorter transverse arm, a quarter, a dime, three pennies for those unexpected evenings when strangers arrive, a novelty garter of pale blue ruffled satin, a 3 x 5 index card on which is typed the recipe for Banana Amaze, two red plastic tiddlywinks, a fireman's helmet, three unrecognizable items for which there seem to be no words, a photograph of a clubfooted man taking a picture of three ten-year-old girls sitting on a lawn, a basketball, the seal, in gold, of some cashiered demon in whom Antonia has long since ceased to believe, a number of erotic letters to Antonia from a correspondent signing himself Pepe, a novelty corkscrew for novelty evenings, a newspaper clipping that tells the story of a wealthy magazine publisher and sportsman who fell into a ditch and claimed the loss of something valuable, a collection of

The interest was definitely growing, slowly

glass stirring rods now almost universally called swizzle sticks, a dish towel stained with some unspeakable liquid, something utterly bewildering, a few more things, an off-print of an article published in *PMLA*

Although there was some shuffling of feet and a few furtive coughs

and entitled "Food Imagery and the English Mystical Tradition: The Role of Bacoun and Eys in Medieval 'Convent Tales,'" an alienating, self-indulgent, and confusing novel by a writer whose name is best forgotten, three disgusting items, the names of which will be graciously omitted, a chart showing the narrative line and plot development of a novel by an author who writes immediate classics about life and its beguiling wonder, a bunch of

Getting thin yet the ever-fruitful imagination

chopsticks for convivial Oriental afternoons, a red candle with the wick cut off, a hoe, a pamphlet issued by the Tribade Conspiracie: "Death to Emily Dickinson's Modesty!," what appears to be a shopping list: milk, bread, eggs, meat? check, cleaners, an unpaid parking summons issued by the Lamoille County Sheriff's Department on the back of which is written "Tonia, is Tues night [unintelligible]," a smooth orange-and-ocher pebble, a warranty card

This gave us all the sense of life as lived in all its beguiling wonder

not filled out, for a battery-powered vibrator to soothe away those tensions, an American

You saw how, as promised, Antonia was gradually becoming more real to

-flag lapel pin, some this and some that, a raffle ticket for a Christmas 1971 drawing at Our Lady of Crushing Sorrows R.C. Church, offered: the usual prizes, led by a twenty-five-pound turkey, a picture postcard of the Golden Gate Bridge

"This had been some goddamned drawer," a voice

taken from the North Bay end, showing the golden city of San Francisco, on the back of which has been crudely lettered in pencil the word cupcakes, a broken-pointed Mongol No. 2 pencil for party use, a copy of Viña Delmar's 1928 novel, *Bad Girl,* a package of three Sheik condoms for those interesting evenings when importunate guests batter at the door, a female puppet named Annette, a photograph of five drunken men each of whom brandishes the exotic confection known as cotton candy, an invitation to a cocktail party at the Mervishes, mercifully unknown, another red candle, with wick, four more

Holy Sweet Mother of God

things that will not bear scrutiny, an India-ink drawing of someone, who even now crunches, crunches in place with unsettling maniacal insistence, and finally, perhaps, finally

A hesitant yet hopeful scattering of applause

it looks as if, yes, one more item, it is the scrap of paper earlier mentioned. It was the scrap of paper stuck in the jointure of the bottom and left sides of the drawer, in the back. A scrap of paper, it was a bit of the margin of a newspaper page, yellowed with age and a good deal of rough party use, on which can be made out, in soft pencil, the word, the single word

Absolutely amazing

beacon, uncanny, certainly more than mere chance, beacon, startling

Startling is right, "Uncanny is more like it," an excited female voice

because, of course, the attentive reader, as well as the rest of you here gathered in the kitchen despite persistent qualms, most of which were understandable if not quite forgivable, you saw that this word, lost in the drawer of a minor figure's kitchen, is the same word that is used for, must we really go on?

"Truly incredible," the same female voice, pitched now

Still, certain of the small crowd seemed more interested in getting to know each other, now that they found themselves thrown together for some obscure literary purpose. We don't know who they are. One thing seemed certain, and that was the relentless marching and crunching in place, outside, as we certainly recalled, on the gravel driveway, of the previously rummaging someone. In the face of everything that had happened, and despite all his expectations, even, we may have said, his sophistication, this discovery stuns him. Perhaps dazed would be more accurate. Stuns and dazed.

Carefully, someone had pulled the brittle and yellowing, or yellowed, scrap of paper from the crack in which it is caught. Rummaging is one thing. This was what he briefly thought of as extracting. He read the single word. He was stunned, dazed. He walked from the kitchen, out the door, onto the gravel driveway, where, surely stunned, and quite possibly dazed, he now trudges blindly toward the street. Toward the road. Toward the car. Open the window. He began eating. It was a dark and louring afternoon. In the late summer of that year he and all the rest of us lived in a house in a village. She was very tired. Shut the door. He looks up slowly.

He crunched, his feet crunch, that is, on the gravel. It was truly amazing, he thinks. He thought earlier. Not now.

"Incredible that Antonia should have concealed this scrap of paper here and nowhere else." Here, that is, there.

It had been a night of restless sleep, haunted by bizarre dreams.

And so we may ponder the mystery, despite the streaming clouds and the constant threat of rain, ever more rain. And we mean rain, not a shower or two. Yes, we may ponder on the mystery of how it has come about or how, earlier, it came about that Antonia, in whom nobody is interested, although she had turned out to be more than a little fascinating now that we've come to know her, how it happens that she seems to have concealed this scrap of paper in such fashion that it can be found, as it has been found, here, in this place, and no other. Now.

Baye tree

Commentary suggests that despite what we think we have discovered, Antonia is alive if not precisely well. And has anyone noticed how like her name is to her husband's? Certain liberties have been taken by the narrator or narrators, agreed. Too many to go into, surely, yet one among them all has twisted and sullied the otherwise adequate scene in the kitchen, or, as it has come to be known, the "kitchen scene." I had personally met Antonia some years before at a real-estate-management convention, a pretty, vibrant young woman whose hair was the color of autumnal aspen leaves.

They choose titles with great care, of course. Yet "Beacon" seems to go a bit too far. "Autumnal aspen leaves." Or "Baye tree." They seem more pertinent if not more credible. We spoke at the hotel bar of many things and I felt her captivating perfume insinuate itself into her halting words. Until, until I was, well, whatever I was. I no longer cared. That night we made love for the first time. The breeze had a welcome edge of autumnal chill to it. Outside, the bay tree insinuated its perfume into the darkest corners of the captivating garden, a garden through which we later walked in a rapt silence. As far as I can recall, now that I look back upon the events of that extraordinary night, the words "Baye tree" were those that had been hurriedly scrawled on the scrap of paper in the kitchen drawer. A mysterious correspondence, yet what was not? Does it seem as if the entire scheme begins to show itself plain? So it would appear.

In her ecstasy, feigned or not, she had cried out a single word that I did not quite catch but which, nevertheless, chilled me to the bone. The curtains floated, ghostly, in the soft wind from the sea. I caught her looking at me as I busied myself at the writing desk, and I let the sweater slip from my lifeless fingers. How blind I had been, blind and stupid and unfeeling.

76

I went to the window.

I stood looking out of the window!

The sweater lay, a crumpled heap, on the floor, and on the lampshade there was caught another garment, a wisp of diaphanous lace.

The bay tree moved, almost imperceptibly, in the freshening wind.

Certainly, I could envision the possibilities, even though there had been nothing that can be called candor employed. Yet the silence of the bar and her oddly amused gaze had permitted me to imagine, if only for a moment, that there might be some authority to what we had otherwise jokingly dismissed as futile, some, but not total. And jokingly? I had been, I confess, the one to use the word, even though it had been manifestly cruel.

There might be some *authority* to what we've otherwise jokingly dismissed, I had said.

As futile? she had replied.

The barman had been listening closely to our conversation and now he walked toward where we sat, knees touching, at the end of the long bar, deserted but for the three of us.

I realized that we were caught in a strangely formal dance, a dance of strangers.

Soon, we were making love, furiously, profligately, unashamedly. It is, even now, somewhat simple to envision the possibilities.

It must be the bay tree, she had sighed. I let my lifeless sweater—or was it her lifeless sweater?—slip from my fingers.

Christmas! I later discovered that Antonia hated it. It had found her, years before, huddled in the shadow of an ancient bay tree that could be seen from any coign of vantage on the sweeping verandah. The lights of the vast living room drenched the windowpanes with a soft rose glow, and the muffled laughter of the guests came sporadically, on the freshening wind, to her ears. But did it matter? It would be difficult, she knew, but there seemed no other way, no alternative to the course she had chosen. She imagined her father at his beloved whist.

She remembers the rest hazily, if at all. But the sound of the cruel ax as it bit relentlessly into the wood of what she had always been assured was her tree is a sound that even now fills her eyes with pain.

Now ye're no better than us! the harsh rural voice cried from the darkness. And then she had drifted into her own darkness.

Yet had I been any less cruel? I had not, indeed, said "ye're," but I had surely, if hesitantly, implored her to let the nagging suppositions rest, to let them disappear, as suppositions must. But had I been formally correct? Had I given credence to the physical reality, to the facts? Had I not been as guilty of a certain velleity in my protestations as had those who once governed her every deed? Had I mocked, rather than comforted, probed, rather than accepted, had I, in short, compromised her innocent and bewildered anger? Most seriously, had I brusquely rearranged the agenda?

There was something sentient about it, something almost human. Its silhouette pierced jaggedly the lightening sky to the east. In the despair and wretchedness of her thwarted longing, I knew that her eyes were fastened on my back, probing for some sign of compassion in the configuration of the body that had, I knew, but used her own. Yet I had felt something akin to love.

Am I, have I been, guilty in your eyes of a certain velleity? I managed. I dared not turn to look at her.

Only insofar as your protestations, she said evenly. They were almost pathetically transparent.

I imagined her brilliant nudity against the soft whiteness of the bedclothes. I had desired her. I still desired her. Still, to think that she had wantonly debased herself with him suffused me with grief and rage, insofar as I could be suffused. Her sweater slipped lifelessly from my fingers and lay in a crumpled heap atop mine.

I dreamt that the bay tree had collapsed, she said later. Shadows moved across the ceiling like mournful wraiths.

Was it my place to tell her that this was but a destructive fantasy? I thought not—I still, God help me, think not—and, looking into her lovely face, I realized that it wasn't the darkness that frightened her. She had been in love, almost, all of her life with darkness. But here, high above the garden and the aromatic bay tree, the darkness seemed, surely, to be not merely a physical manifestation of the mundane, but the absolute harbinger of the dead, still past. How I longed to reassure her! Of what? I thought bitterly.

It was then, I think, that I noticed the credenza. Antonia had seen it as soon as we had entered the room and I realized that her initial modesty in undressing had been occasioned by its dark, burnished presence, there, next to the writing desk. Had I known it then? Known it and chosen to ignore it? Her peach-colored silk slip lay crumpled in soft folds on its glistening surface.

Can you hand me my slip? she cried softly from the bathroom. But the dawn would not come! Only the cold wind soughing through the leaves of the bay tree testified to my actuality. What, then, was the name of the garment caught impotently on the lampshade? I suddenly felt afraid, as if I had been the chosen receptacle of an unassuaged and acerb grief, causeless and infinite.

Despite what others have said in the course of callous interrogations, Antonia was, for just the space of those few hours, wholly joyous again.

I went to the window, pulling my sweater over my exhausted body. The shower was running and the credenza seemed innocuous in the weak sun that filtered through the drawn curtains, through which I peered at the bay tree. Or was it, finally, the Baye tree? And why had I refused to open the curtains?

Now, of course, but too late, much too late for it to matter, I feel the nagging doubts. Was it indeed that her name seemed but a monumental parody of her husband's? Perhaps. Or perhaps it was someone else with some other name, someone else who was so inextricably involved, given the obsessions of the narrator, or narrators. And they were obsessions, inevitable perhaps, perhaps even forgivable, yet present, eternally, obstinately present. I cannot help but feel that they have created the chimera of the fiasco in the kitchen, a fiasco that occurred, despite every effort, years later. But then, I had immediately taken notice of the striking young woman who entered the hotel bar, alone, her subdued but flattering dress, her modest demeanor, the perfectly coiffed scintillance of her shining black hair.

They have said "Beacon," they have suggested "Shadowie lumpe," they have all but insisted on "Baye tree." For me, these are but stage properties, although I have admittedly spoken, for what seems a lifetime, out of a persistent remorse, biting if virtually nameless, and almost painfully acerb. We chatted easily of the afternoon's dull lectures and I found myself drawn ineluctably toward her. Was it the oddly bizarre scent of her perfume? Or do I now comfort myself with that mundane possibility? I spoke smoothly, even, I confess, glibly, into the mystery of her eyes, yet felt inert as some large piece of furniture, perhaps a credenza. It was but the matter of a few moments, or so I remember it, until we were in bed together, lost in each other's arms, and legs. The soft wind from the sea carried the penetrant and familiar aroma of the bay tree, far below, into our darkened room. Despite my most powerful efforts, I came to realize, if not willingly to accept, that the scrap of paper in what she had tearfully admitted was, indeed, her kitchen drawer, had had roughly inscribed on it the words "Baye tree." Not even our languid stroll through the hotel gardens could assist me in denying the remarkably curious turn that things had taken, *general* things. I had begun to see the heretofore dim form of the overall plan growing clear. Now, of course, I know that I neglected—or was it that I refused?—to perform those actions that would have changed everything. But at the time, close to her, intoxicated with various aromas, I thought, I knew—nothing.

In the abandonment of her passion she had whispered a name into the darkness, a name that I recognized, yet did not recognize. It has haunted me all these years, and yet, at the time, I had not the temerity to ask Antonia precisely who it was that she had named. While she slept, or seemed to sleep, I pottered idly with the stationery in the writing desk, but then stopped, knowing without having to turn that her eyes were following my every move. I let a postcard slip from my lifeless fingers. Was this, then, to be all?

I went to the closet. I entered. There were the hangers, I thought angrily.

What was it that had permitted all this to come to pass as it had come to pass? I was not yet so incapable of human feeling as to be unable to imagine the possible conjunctions of this liaison, its potential inevitabilities. Even though there had been nothing that can be called precipitate action on either of our parts, there was a stillness, a reality about the ultimate reasons for this strange state that was, or soon would be, or so I feared, isomorphic in its perfection. Was there some mundane, some obvious cause for the combinatory elements that had, seemingly, come out of nowhere?

I had re-entered the dim room, and addressing the dark shape on the bed, noted, There may well be, I think, something isomorphic in the strange perfection of this night.

But has it, she began, then caught her breath. I waited near the closet.

Has it what? I said.

Has it a—mundane cause? she whispered.

Earlier, the barmaid had vulgarly adjusted her brassiere, listening, all the while, to our subtly erotic verbal fencing. I have come to judge this act as a sexual metonym, but at the time had not the confidence to articulate my beliefs.

Antonia had so easily broken through my somewhat puritanical barriers, and soon we were lost, blind and wild in our passions, throughout which she had insisted on wearing her shoes. It is still puzzling to me. Had this been done at my behest, or with my permission? Or was permission but moot in such a sudden conjunction? Nevertheless, it had been so.

The bay tree is dying, she had whispered, again. A postcard, the same postcard, slipped lifelessly from my fingers and fluttered helplessly to the floor. It was a sign.

A sign of more to come!

January. A month which filled Antonia with terror, or so I discovered later, had found her, while still a girl, dozing serenely in the shade of the venerable bay tree that had dominated Old Weskit, the family estate, for centuries. It could be seen, this legendary tree, from any place on the grounds, lest one stood behind one of the many buildings that graced the lush acreage. Her mother was at the spinet, pretending to play, while her father gazed out toward what he'd stubbornly demanded be called the tree line. The truth about it, and about so many other things, had come to her the night before, yet she was, as she now admitted, utterly passive in the face of what she dreaded would be the final blow. She could see, in her mind's eye, her mother's delicate fingers twitching gracefully in the air just above the keys of the heirloom instrument. She knew.

The next few weeks, or months, passed as if in a restless dream, yet the terrible *chunk* of the ax against the trunk of the bay tree recurs again and again in her memory.

Now d' ye think ye're better'n us? the harsh voice mocked from the darkness. And then came the darkness of blessed oblivion.

But I, too, had been harsh, as well as abrupt. And though I had couched my questions and replies in the most courteous terms, wasn't it also my responsibility at least to assist in the balance of what I now see were the perorations? The rhetoric, yes, that goes without saying. I had no reason to malign my motives as far as that was concerned. But what of the varied innuendoes? The sentences that trailed off? What of the tortuous clusterings of gossip and snide half-truths? Had I lied by omission? Had I, that is, tyrannically rearranged otherwise simple strategies?

I had known, for a moment, love. Of that I was reasonably sure. Yet, when I looked awkwardly out the window, the bay tree seemed wounded, and, yes, dying. Although I instantly entered the closet again, the closet with its hangers!, I felt that her eyes were boring into my soul.

I re-entered the room, trembling.

Does the rhetoric, at least, go without saying? I had asked.

The rhetoric? she said quietly. Yes, the rhetoric. Her voice trailed off into soft breathing, then:

But not the innuendoes! she cried. Her body was a dazzling, shimmering white in the darkness. I wanted her, as, now, I still want her. But she had deceived me as she had deceived all the others, especially him. I threw the postcard from me and watched it flutter into a corner of the lifeless room.

Later, after we had slept, she suddenly murmured, I dreamt that the by tree . . . spoke to me.

The by tree? I replied.

There was a long silence during which I looked at her impassive face, and fought against the temptation to tell her, even as I knew that such a confession might well be considered only a kind of moral gesture at what, at that time, I was pleased to think of as the infinite. Now, such a theory merely brings a wry smile to my lips. I thought that her remote, trancelike air might be the result of the sound of the foghorns, groaning in their timeless melancholy, or the barely discernible ringing of the bell buoys far out in the angry wash of the relentless swells. Yet the monstrous silhouette of the tortured bay tree was nowhere near the cliff's edge! For a moment, I thought that she might not be able to go on, but I knew that she would go on, would live with the unassuaged grief that gave her no rest, no peace. The darkness was implacable and in its grip our desire reawakened. I wanted to make love to her again—again and again and again! But my near-frenzied groping on the floor for her shoes was, as I suspected it would be, fruitless.

Then, the credenza loomed. I had seen it from the corner of my eye as we had earlier tremblingly begun to undress each other, but it had not, then, actually loomed. Antonia had finished disrobing in the closet, so she, too, had noticed its persistent presence. Why had I not? Or had I? Had I, and, as usual, cravenly denied the warnings of my heart? Her peach-colored silk slip shimmered on the polished surface. So that's where it had gone! I felt the blood rush to my temples. *Will* you *please* hand me my slip? she cried from the bathroom. Would this night never end? Was it only the coarse action of the barmaid that had called into being the *actuality* of my self? Was it on such ephemera that my tenuous grasp on what she had rather crudely called entelechy rested? So it appeared, at least then. Yet to what could I assign the fact that a nameless garment of feminine apparel lay beneath the slip? I thought, for a feverish moment, that I was not I, and that she was not she, but that we were—some other people!

But who?

I have, since that time, firmly denied, in the face of all queries, that this was, or even might have been, so.

Nonetheless, and if other reports are given even partial credence, we had sounded the depths of a profound *jouissance* that night.

I could hear her humming sadly to herself as she began her toilet, and I pulled my clothes on as rapidly and noiselessly as possible. No small feat! Banging my knee painfully on the sharp edge of the looming credenza, I made my way out of the room. The bay tree shimmered mysteriously in the moonlight.

I had reached the house, and reconnoitering so as to avoid the man whose faint footsteps I had heard crunching on the gravel of the driveway, I somehow effected an entrance into the kitchen.

There was the drawer.

There was the scrap of paper, still caught within it. Had I always known what I would read thereon? Sometimes, even now, I think so.

Now, you have it. It is precisely now, and here. Just so.

Baye tree.

Rocke

But it is not lost, clearly, since he is looking at an old sepia-tone photograph of Sheila although he doesn't know but only assumes or pretends is better, pretends that this is Sheila, he has never known Sheila, she is dressed in a pepper-and-salt tweed country suit, sitting on a large flat rock, posed on a large flat rock, in the center of a field, somewhere, he pretends to himself as he looks at the photograph that this girl is his wife, or was his wife, although he has no idea why, he has no wife, he had no wife, there is something odd and essentially unconvincing about the photograph, rooted in the fact, the fact?, that Sheila or his wife seems out of place, assuming that she has or had a place, and, as it were, out of costume, if such a plain garment can be called a costume, in all the years that he knew her, or pretended to know her, or is now pretending that he knew her, for years, he never saw her in anything so severe, so, if you will, chaste, although he must admit, or he may as well admit, here, where better a place, that he heard, many times, from various lovers, and read, more than once, in passages of prose purporting to be true, that is, based on facts, facts?, concerning her, remarks by her husband, her real husband, Lou, who is, who was, based on other characters, other people, supposedly actual, that she always wore white underwear, if Lou can be trusted, not always, but he knows, he thinks, what always means, and what Lou means, and he may wish to consider these latter garments as chaste, or representative of chastity, as Lou did not, or he may not so wish to consider them as such,

he may not so wish to consider them as such, it so happens that, a nice phrase, useful to the writer of what he decides should be, or shall be, called a tale, the girl, Sheila, in the photograph, is Sheila at eighteen, or perhaps only seventeen, and it also may so happen that the Sheila he knew, or pretended to know, or didn't know at all, is not the girl who seems out of place in this field, this reproduction, this image, of a field, and that this is the reason that she seems so unconvincing, since the actual Sheila would never wear such a severe, or chaste, tweed suit, therefore this photo is of someone who is pretending to be Sheila, or someone very like her, whoever she may be, or may have been, or may not have been, the field is autumnal, as he has noted, but not here, surely not here, he can check that easily enough, the girl, who, given the date on which the photograph was taken, is no longer a girl, has a face that is striking, as striking as it was when he first met her, or pretended to etcetera, etcetera, and her legs, although covered by her skirt, to some three inches below her knees, which are modestly pressed together, are as beautiful in the photo as they were described as being, by someone, in some tale, there's the word, as beautiful as when he, as someone or other, someone with a name, a meticulous history, history is necessary to understand prose, not all of it, some of it, as beautiful as that time when he first stared at them, rather shamelessly, at a ridiculous party to which he had gone to celebrate the publication of a book, another book, yet another book written for some reason, the world seems to be full of writers,

full of writers, yet despite that depressing fact, fact?, time has a way, another trenchant phrase, it has a way of exaggerating the beauty of innumerable things, including the legs of women, that has the ring of authority, a trenchant phrase with the ring of authority, of surety, a kind of absolute sense of, of declaration, something like a motto, or a maxim, or perhaps a bromide, or, to be unkind, as he often is, a cliché, which latter word he does not flinch from, he is thinking of being a writer, or, if not a writer, of writing, of adding some babble to the present babble, and why not?, he says aloud, in the best literary tradition of speaking aloud, to the walls, to the window, to his feet, to, if he wishes, his ass, as he rises from his desk, there is even a desk, and looks out the window at, it may as well be, at the traffic far below, not, it will be confessed, a bad place for traffic to be in a tale, or while still sitting here, or there, at his desk, perhaps he was, or is, he gets himself away from the window to give the tenses a chance, merely thinking of writing a brief paragraph or two, on himself, more or less himself, looking at a photograph of Sheila, he now calls her Sheila, perhaps, that may well be the case, that may well be it, he can't see that it makes any difference, Sheila, fine, yet

Sheila always despised the country, dulcius urbe quid est?, she might have said, probably not, yet that's the ticket, or was, that's her motto or is it bromide?, so what is she doing here, on a flat rock, in a tweed suit, he looks again, or thinks of himself looking again, at something, at the photograph, of course, the photograph, which is absent, which may be merely a handy device around which he can write his tale, or his paragraph, or paragraphs, an entry into the truth, or something, a way of being able to write rock, field, photograph, and as he does this, looks, imagines, writes, he perceives, perceives is good, he perceives that Sheila's legs, those imagined legs, were not really as beautiful as the legs of this Sheila, in the photograph, or in the word, photograph, this girl in the imagined field in the photograph on his imagined desk,

on his imagined desk, Sheila rises from the rock, stretches and yawns, now he can get a good look at her legs, she vigorously brushes her skirt, she moves slowly to the window, to gaze at the traffic, no, she brushes her skirt with her hands, to rid it of dust, dirt, twigs, other things, country things, perhaps she lights a cigarette, if she smokes, she rummages through, or in, her bag, he is, in effect, spying on her, odd how the photograph has come alive, or something, he'll find the phrase later, he spies on her, he waits for her to do something important, something fit to be set down, so that he may discover for his readers, his readers to come, more or less, the truth about something, about life, life will do, he says to himself, life, excellent, in the smallest actions which one makes one's little word-puppets perform one, of course, always discovers, for someone, the truth, about life, he waits, she may do something exciting, something that will enable him to understand the, erotic flush, he writes, or soon will write, that pervaded his body, or certain parts of it, he is nothing, he knows, if not accurate, or is it comic, on that certain afternoon, years ago, when he and Sheila, let's say, this old one, or that new one, although new is not precisely the word, he'll attend to precision later, or that one in the absent photograph, he is having trouble now following the figure, or the trope, the literary something, he'll attend to it all, later, that afternoon, when he and she sat drinking cognac, in the private bar of somebody's house, a rich man's house, on Long Island, in, in Locust Valley, the name comes to him, as a reasonable locale, and the young woman, this Sheila, or that Sheila, or the other Sheila, still near the rock, or so he thinks, the young woman is definitely Sheila, now, despite the name, or names, she may have borne in other tales, there's the word again, it's all made up, or was, but now, or soon, it will be based, however, to be sure, on what he now calls, real life, although he doesn't actually call, names, that's more like what he does, he names it real, then adds, life, it will be based on that afternoon when she stretched her long and remarkably well-made legs out before him, so that he couldn't take his eyes off them, succinct, all right, those legs belonging to, to her, but not to, he decides, the Sheila who is, now, strangely moving around in the photograph, or, even more strangely, moving around in the word, photograph,

in the word, photograph, Sheila sits again, this tale is at a far remove from the exciting, she sits, she pretends, he pretends that she pretends, that she is only seventeen, or eighteen, and not what she is, now, whatever she is, he figures rapidly, let's make it forty-five, or, he'll make it forty-five, when he writes his tale, based, of course, on etcetera, etcetera, she sits, she begins to do some, some thinking, she cannot stand, despite the age she is, for the moment, trapped in, she cannot stand Lou, Lou will do fine, she cannot stand Lou, he remembers Lou, nor can she stand her lovers, whose ranks he may join, if he writes the tale, or even the paragraph, or two, for truth will out, more or less, usually less, usually not at all, for that matter, for if the truth outs, an awkward phrase, he'll fix that up later, if it does, it will be revealed that her lovers bore her with their pleas, their needs, they call them needs, only on occasion, give the devil his due, he calls them needs, but he, as he sits at his desk, or even while away from it, he is a, a, traditionalist, preferring, above all other things, meaningful things to occur to characters whom we, he usually thinks this we, meaning, he supposes, us, whom we can care about, making order out of chaos is his middle name, or soon will be, if he realizes his fondest dream, of writing, of writing the truth, they bore her, they all want, want, want and demand, things, from her, what things, he is presently too lazy to discover, there he is at the window again, and there, below, is the fucking traffic, they want things, they give her interesting roles to play, she enters, she exits, she plays the unfaithful wife, she is, Sheila is, she turns out to be Sheila, after all, she is, indeed, the unfaithful wife, he has her pretend to pretend to think this, as she taps a cigarette on her fingernail, he has given her a whole pack, minus one, of course, put it into the bag in which she rummaged, is still rummaging, forever, in that deathless sentence, she taps, he decides, Sheila taps a cigarette on her thumbnail, a nice touch, a nice piece of business, in the elaborate piece of business that her life has become, another nice, another cleanly turned, an inventive phrase, he used to think he knew the word for the figure, perhaps conceit, metaphor, vehicle, no, in any event it is, indeed, something literary, to permit him, or somebody, so to transform, or transcend life in order that it be made understandable, that's how art works, though he realizes that it is hard to understand life from a photograph, especially an imagined photograph, a real photograph to be referred to is much more effective, as a device, for understanding, for making sense of, of what?, of life, even though it displays a woman, who, it may well be, was the girl who might well have become his wife, before he met her, at, seventeen, or eighteen, yet this woman, too, hated the country, her name, her name was Sheila, an odd coincidence, that's life, or is it an irony?, there is something to be made of that, so he thinks, as he gazes, as he stares, blankly, as he is attracted to, blankly?, as he stares, blankly, at the typewriter, he has a typewriter, a desk, and a typewriter, the room is slowly being furnished, the wonder of literature, at the typewriter, yes, and at the yellow legal pad, as he turns from the window, as he does this, as he does that, blankly, as he lights a cigarette, and realizes, once again, as he has been taught, by something, call it literature, experience, the anxiety of looking at that blank piece of paper, the intimidating presence of, how lonely it is, how lonely he is, as if anyone asked him, he can go fuck himself with his anxiety, and his paragraphs, and his photograph, more or less,

more or less a photograph anyway, and now he sees, he speaks figuratively, he's willing to say so, again, not actually say it, he is silent, he realizes, that's a little better, that his life, no, that he has fallen into the trap that he thought, or had thought, or will eventually think, at that anxious moment, before the time-honored, the famous blank sheet of paper, to avoid, he is turning Sheila into a figure, an element, a thing, really, to be caught in a chain of metaphor, that sounds like the right phrase, but she is no such thing, she is flesh, and blood, well, flesh and blood, so to speak, she is a picture, a part of a picture, no, part of a photograph, no, the word, photograph, there is probably no photograph, although he seemed to be looking, at something on his desk, he definitely still has a desk then, but it is a strange photograph, absent, since she is, well, she is moving around in the photograph, he is looking out the window, staring, no, gazing, out the window, out a window, not at the wonderful goddamned traffic, time-tested, far below, but at the field, a field, that has at its center, more or less at its center, a rock, and so forth, and so on, in any event, she is no such girl, or woman, as she here exists, that is doubtlessly the fact, the fact?, that he must face, well, not must face, that he faces, she is Sheila, so it is Sheila, after all, in a tweed suit, underneath which, is Lou's white underwear, he calls it Lou's, but it is not actually Lou's, by Lou's he means, etcetera, maybe it is white, maybe not, he will not, at this time, undress her, although he has the power to do so, she is at his mercy, so he thinks, or he has himself think, that's always good, a neat way into the mind, thinking, mind is an odd word to use, in this context, so is context, in this context, what context can he be thinking of?, he thinks, or wonders, he has no context, at present, he has that blank, that lonely, that etcetera, Sheila is on the rock again, her cigarette is finished, she is beginning to feel cold, and why not?, the sun, weirdly enough, is going down, it is actually, more or less, actually sinking, right here, or there, in the photograph, real, or imagined, or projected, in any case, the sun is sinking, and Sheila, despite her tweed suit, which is warm, is beginning to feel cold, she is cold, right here, or there, in her tweed suit, her warm tweed suit, that's how it works out, in literature, because it's an oxymoron, or a litotes, and maybe the wind is coming up,

the wind is coming up, and that, for some reason, allows him to know that she hasn't had an orgasm, with Lou, he'll stick with Lou, so that's decided, although there are plenty of other names available, dozens of them, hundreds, Sidney, for instance, or Kirk, Gig, Mickey, endless, but Lou will do nicely, he knows that Lou is not the real name of the real Sheila's real husband, the name that the name, Lou, was meant to conceal, in the tale in which he first met Lou, under, a curious word, under another name, which he has forgotten, or has pretended to forget, how strange to meet people in tales, or is it?, he has no idea, or no ideas, he merely wants to write, to forge in the city of his soul a blank etcetera, more fool he, write his own tale, Sheila, however, despite all, has not had an orgasm, with Lou, in almost seven years, which seems fine to him, not to Lou, that will make her twenty-four or twenty-five, if her age, in the photograph, is right, though he has the nagging sense, another smooth, another familiar phrase, that he has somehow figured wrong, he doesn't care, or rather, I don't care, he says, to the window?, to the window, out the window, he says, aloud, but he denies, give him credit, he denies himself the window, the traffic, the blank stare, Jesus Christ, enough is enough, a hell of a guy, yet, where was he?, yet, she has often pretended to have an orgasm, or orgasms, a few, or many, he knows that Lou knows that she is, or has been, pretending, and that he is faintly pleased, at her groans, her grunts, her sighs, her gasps, it's good enough for Lou, and if it's good enough for Lou, it's good enough for him, if the truth were known, back again, to the known truth, literature allows the truth to be known, it is the writer's function to etcetera, he should admit, once and for all, that the truth is known, for Sheila has spoken to him, from the rock, in the field, wearing her etcetera, while the cold and so on, she has spoken the words he has wished her to speak, whatever they are, he doesn't give a shit what they are, even though she is bored, by now, with this field, and, as he knows, as he has created it, as he has thought of creating it, it is cold, and so is Sheila, for the wind, etcetera,

the wind, etcetera, etcetera, and as he looks at the photograph again, he now says, with authority, with confidence, the idiot, photograph, he now insists that he has a photograph, it's little enough, when he looks at it again, or, since it is now unimpeachably here, as it was not heretofore necessarily here, at all, when he looks at it, for the first time, or, as if for the first time, assuming that it was here, or there, all along, and why should we doubt him?, or it, or this?, he is mildly surprised to discover that it is a sepia-tone photograph, in which Sheila, it is indeed still Sheila, a girl of seventeen, or eighteen, who looks remarkably like his invented wife, the one given him, or taken by him, he is not one to deny free will, in some tale he was once, as it is said, in, as somebody whose name he no longer remembers, or whose name he does not care to remember, or pretends he does not care to remember, even though the tale has been spoken of as unforgettable, as a minor classic, Sheila is standing, against a tree, of some undetermined species, a tree bare of leaves, a gaunt, gaunt is good, a gaunt tree, a look of absolute defiance on her face, one hand thrust into a pocket of her tweed jacket, rather elegantly, so that the position of her hand, and arm, reminds him,

somewhat disconcertingly, of a photograph, of a bridegroom, which he
once saw, and which proves nothing, except for the unwholesome, or
something, nature of partial, perhaps specious, recall, her expression is
that of the woman with whom he drank cognac, that afternoon in Locust
Valley, right, an expression at once defiant, as noted, strong, bitter,
daring, sexual, for it turns out, so it turns out, it happens, that someone,
it is Lou, Lou is at the door, there must be a door, Lou is asking, Lou
asked, if she would like to join the gang, that's what Lou calls the rest of
the guests, he assumes that there are guests, he had no idea, until now,
that there was anybody else in the house, what house?, well, the
assumed house, but there is, it appears, a gang of them, mysterious
indeed are the powers of literature, powers that permit them to hide,
somewhere, until needed, would she, Lou asks, or asked, like to join the
rest of the gang, in making jack-o'-lanterns, a nice touch, observant,
lifelike, yet uncommon, the darkness is falling, the darkness is gathering
behind, or beyond, is better, beyond the huge picture window, that
looks out on fields, and woods, dropping off to a brilliant shard of, a
shining slice of, something, water, he will write, soon, perhaps, water,
although it seems to be the Connecticut River, but what the hell does he
care what it is?, he will maybe write, though, the Connecticut River,
visible through the gold and yellow and crimson trees, that is, the leaves
are golden and etcetera, it is an autumnal scene, much like the one in the
photograph, although the colors as here carefully denoted, can only, in
the photograph, be imagined, and that, only if the gaunt trees therein are
given back their leaves, of various colors, to prove, in order to prove,
something, as if he gives a fuck, one detail is as good as another, when
truth, he says, aloud, is the goal, and so on and so forth, that's his motto
or his paradigm, or is it his hypotaxis?, whatever, Sheila sips her
cognac, then raises her free hand, lets it fall, lets it rest, gently, relaxed,
on his upper thigh, he sees that Lou sees this, sees that Lou stares, with
a bitter yet unsurprised look on his face, then turns and leaves, he will,
he might, have him do something to enrich the poignancy of the scene,
he calls it, in his mind, a scene, and if a scene, why not a poignant one,
he will, or might, make Lou whistle, a small touch, perceptive, an
insight into the vagaries of human nature, a wonderful and smoothly
administered dash of literary something or other, literary bullshit,
bullshit is not bad, though a trifle crass, a trifle vulgar, a correlative for

bleak despair, now he's got it, yet, and yet, he remembers Lou whistling, as he leaves, his hands thrust, but not elegantly, into the pockets of his worn corduroys, worn is a judiciously selected adjective, he feels, he felt, so he thinks, so he writes, or will write, sorry for Lou, but he wants, or wanted, Sheila, who will later tell him that she despises those corduroys, he will not ask why, as well as that melodramatic whistling, even though he was, is, will be, the one responsible for it, just as well she doesn't know,

she doesn't know, Sheila, now, that is, then, at the time of the photograph, he continues to insist on this object, or this word, a girl of seventeen or eighteen, she, now, who reminds him of his invented wife, as if he had an invented wife, some word, that's more like it, an unabashed word, that's the ticket, that's the way to go, she, whoever she is, Sheila, the word is sitting, now, or was sitting, on a flat rock, in the middle of a field, of the field, in the photograph, in reality, reality will have to do, in an autumnal field, the crimsons and the golds, the yellows, the russets, too, and so on, the wind, and so forth, it seems to be getting a little chilly, and etcetera, another shot at the fucking scene, perhaps he'll get it, perfectly, the perfect scene, beautifully done, evocative, that's good, probing, revelatory, yes, that's the ticket, same ticket as before, she is still fumbling in her bag, she has fumbled, as he knows, she is, right, smoking a cigarette, perhaps the same cigarette, he discovers that there is an oddly lascivious smile, on her face, perhaps not so odd, a smile that husbands often think they see, on the faces of other men's wives, more fools they, these smiling women, these wives, a few of them anyway, at least one or two of them, maybe one of them, and that on rare occasions, he is about to write, as he paces, as he sharpens his pencil, as he looks out, etcetera, on and on and on, with this and with that, these smiling women, he insists on more than one, seem to be thinking, as if they, as if they something, no, as they chat, about children, about jobs, about the banalities of politics, about their husbands' jobs, that they would be delighted, simply delighted, to permit their conversational partners, or partner, he has been a partner, somewhere, as if that mattered, that they would be more than pleased to permit him, the partner, who may still be listening to the sound of whistling, growing ever fainter, that's nicely turned, that's warmly familiar, permit him the most remarkable, the most unbridled, wanton, and lustful liberties, that's a mouthful,

a mouthful, so that quickly he turns to, he hears a train, in the distance, why not?, the good old lonesome sound, of a train, what a wonder, he notices, once again, as always, he is observant, as all good writers must be, perhaps not all, somebody said, somebody is still saying, probably the same somebody who said, who says, that good writers must also be, also be something, good listeners, right, listeners to what, or to whom, and for what reason, is never, wait, was never explained, perhaps it was, or is, bad writers who must be good listeners, but he notices, and has noticed, for some time, whatever that means, in the upper-left quadrant of the photograph, a railroad-crossing sign, how handily it has appeared, its reality is, what?, winning?, that's not it, he doesn't care, and this word, Sheila, of course, Sheila, she's still here, or there, this Sheila who reminds him of, right, she is still smiling her oddly lascivious smile, as some wives do, when etcetera, etcetera, she looks toward where the tracks, in reality, reality will have to do, must be, that is, he cannot see them in the photograph, the imagined photograph, what an imagination he has, it's of course a necessity, like observing, and listening, he thinks to comment on this to someone, soon, perhaps a friend, he will soon have, maybe, a friend, or somebody's wife, not his own, he has no wife, nor did he ever, yet with his imaginative powers, or with somebody's imaginative powers, you never can tell, you never can tell, she looks, she rises from her chair, she rises abruptly, she goes to the window, here's the picture window, good as new, to look at the fields, the woods, the trees, the riot of colors, nature's great palette, breathtaking autumn, yet somehow, somehow something, somehow sad, right, sad autumn, another handy phrase, just waiting, just waiting to help the imagination out, she looks down, or away, to the shining slice of river beyond, the brief glint, the silvery glitter, Jesus, the shining slice, the brief glint of its cold waters, all right, he smiles, at the traffic, no, at his desk, or he aims, he aims a smile at, no, he looks at her legs, her thighs, her hips, her buttocks, her breasts, all perfect, beneath her closely fitting, yet not immodest, knitted dress, a wheat-colored dress, no, maize, no, white, he can still feel her hand, on his thigh, it was relaxed, her hand, he would like her permission, and Lou's, he's come to like him, a little, he'll get to like him more, perhaps, as he develops, right, develops his character, he'll grow to respect him, to care about him, he must never be better than his characters, never, that's a rule, he would like, anyway, permission, from somebody, from his imagined wife, in the tale, some tale, the wife who reminded him, of Sheila, or was it the other way around?, he would be grateful, for permission to take liberties, lustful, wanton, and unbridled, with her, but such permission will not be granted, how come?, he is irritated, he drinks, or he drank, some more cognac, Sheila looks down, she looks over the glorious etcetera, the russets, right, the sad autumnal this and that, he decides to have him decide to be ashamed of his obscene desires,

obscene desires, yet, Sheila, Sheila is staring, with a strangely hopeful, he seems to remember that it was hopeful, or strange, some-thing, she has that look, on her face, he is interested, now, only in the facts, the facts?, of this day, of that day, that is, of this photograph, he has decided will be the device, the device whereby he will get at the truth, or something, whereby he will allow his imagination to ferret out the this and the that, she is staring, he pretends to forget the expression, the look, on her face, which looks, looks, curiously hopeful, or was it curiously strange, or lascivious, oddly older, than what?, seventeen or eighteen, she is staring, at the railroad tracks, there they are again, right as rain, those next to the actual, the real, real will have to do, railroad-crossing sign, in the imagined photograph, imagination is all, he thinks, he has him think, with an abstracted, an intense look, on his face, and then he thinks, with a pang, of what?, of remorse, of the crimsons, the blues, no, the golds, the sad, the poignant, the cognac, to which he must ultimately give a name, specificity is a sign of something, perhaps of careful listening, or respect for one's characters, there is something about the train that he hears approaching, and that Sheila hears, something that, illogically, for a change, a refreshing change, and that something, as Sheila knows, now that she is almost forty-five years of age, at last, at long last, is that the train means itself, nothing else, which accounts, perhaps, for her strange, or odd expression, her strangely odd expression, she waits for him to decide, more fool she, she waits for him to let her know, what to think, about this approaching train, in the way that she waited for him to comment, on her legs, her thighs, etcetera, and to comment on Lou, on his corduroys, that are, that were, that will be, worn, pants that she, wait a minute, that she will despise, despised, that she despises, that was some time ago, or something, she is waiting for him to take the most illicit pleasures, etcetera, to seduce her in the guise of some ideal, to say whatever he will say, but it wasn't, apparently, worth the trouble, since she is still waiting, it is growing colder, it must be growing darker, time marches on, but all he does is stand at the window, light another cigarette, a famous literary cigarette, so he thinks of writing, soon, as he lights his cigarette, he thinks, of her body, beneath her pepper-and-salt tweed suit, he thinks, that her body must be as remarkable as her body,

as her body, Sheila's, still here, or, that is, there, on a flat rock, in a field, the photograph, he calls it, he'll not give an inch, has arrested her, in a casual, yet inward, whatever that means, pose, she is about seventeen or eighteen, there, while here, she is about forty-five, here?, a train, the train, there it is, it rushes past, noise, dust, other odds and ends, other words, some three-hundred yards, to her right, to his left, given the position of the absent photograph, whose presence he insists on,

he insists on, why not?, the photograph, and the train, not quite in the photograph, absent, yes, but intensely imagined, imagination is all, or a great deal, and the train has on board, so he decides to discover, a man, whom he will subsequently, maybe, call Tom, or Dick, or Harlan, but not Lou, of course, not Lou, Tom is staring fixedly, such turns of phrase, out the window, at the sad, the autumnal, the poignant, fields, as they rush, as is their wont, by, and at the etcetera, until Tom, Tom will do, sees a young woman, who, he thinks, he has Tom think, who is Sheila, he has almost managed to forget her, how it coheres, Tom stares at Sheila, all seems extraordinarily, to Tom, unreal, as well it might, theatrical, perhaps amazing, maybe, he says aloud, once again, amazing, since the young woman, on etcetera, wearing etcetera, surrounded by sad and poignant etcetera, looks exactly, or very much like, his, Tom's, wife, Janet, this time Tom speaks aloud, what's sauce for the goose, or like Janet when she was seventeen or eighteen, for Janet has, and often, for some obscure reason, of her own, for not much is known, of Janet, shown Tom a photograph, of herself, taken years before, posed, strangely smiling, wearing a well-cut tweed suit, on a rock, in a field, in Connecticut, or so she says, has said, except that Janet is now forty-five years of age, as if that follows,

if that follows, he doesn't care, but the train passes, it rushes, Sheila looks briefly up at it, with an oddly something smile, or look, so he descries, nice word, with some expression, on her face, and in the photograph, that he wishes he now had, assuming that there is a real, real will have to do, photograph, so that he might verify his, his conjectures, his rambling conjectures, with incontestable evidence of, of whatever, it is difficult, given the photograph that he insists he once had, or wrote that he had, but has no longer, for him to make out the intent of this, or that, not quite formed smile, yet he stares, he props the photograph of Sheila, of that word, props the word of the word, up against a brass figurine, of Durga, the goddess, which figurine once appeared in a photograph taken, of another woman, whose name he forgets, although he can look it up, the goddess is on his desk, or, he coughs apologetically, nicely turned, right, it is actually a table, the truth is always best, and he thinks, or notes that he will be thinking, when the time comes, that Durga is a goddess of destruction,

a goddess of destruction, this may be a transcendent analogy, a figure located somewhere on the axis of selection, if it's good enough for etcetera, in any event, he knows, that in the tale that he will invent, or is, at this moment, not actually at this moment, actually will have to do, about Sheila, the Sheila in the photograph, he calls the word photograph photograph, why not?, what else?, yet another thing, perhaps spurious, but not without merit, that the photograph reminds him of one taken of his mother, a sepia-tone photograph, another coincidence to complicate the plot, and it is a plot, and nothing but plot, although he remembers, not the photograph, but the emotion that the photograph evoked in him, but what emotion?, perhaps not emotion, but a sense, of the, of the uncanny, that may be the word, that may be what was evoked, by the photograph, of his mother, unless it is, or was, the uncanny that is, or was, evoked by the photograph, of Sheila, she may as well be Sheila, he cannot recall any face at all, except for the one that is here, or that was there, precision is the first rule, of something, and that face is, always, oddly, the strangely smiling face of Sheila,

the strangely smiling face of Sheila, he thinks, he knows, well, he pretends, that Sheila is unaware, that she does not know what will happen to her, over the course of the next few years, or more than a few, neither is Janet aware, whoever she is, or was, Sheila has not yet heard of Lou, at least he doesn't think she has, he can check, although Lou is, was, the man of the gang, the pants, the pumpkins, pumpkins?, but that came later, later?, or it will come later, in terms of real, have to do, have to do, life, now, Sheila looks at the train, rattling, rushing, still at it, an exotic scene, well, bittersweet, this cannot, despite the evidence of the absent photograph, possibly be Sheila, or his wife, what wife?, some forgotten word, he gazes out the window, he'll give himself a pipe, might as well, in a minute Sheila, this, or that tweedy Sheila, who looks very much like Janet, who is insistent indeed, may well have a brief affair, with Fred, who died, recently, who was, who was an, an accountant, or a master sergeant, or a teacher in Detroit, or who is settling, at the time of the photograph, into a seat behind Tom, Tom, who is looking out the window, at what, at Janet, not Janet, but Sheila, yet Tom is startled because etcetera, and at the sad and russet etcetera, the golds,

the golds, the crimsons, he would like to, he considers rescuing Sheila, from her rock, he calls it hers, from the artificiality, of the scene, scene will have to do, and then burn the photograph, the photograph that he has pretended to prop up, against the goddess Durga, there are metaphorical possibilities, but she is forty-five years of age, not Durga, his mother is dead, many people are dead, they die, and die, and Janet, well, he thinks, vulgarly, fuck Janet, although there she is, more or less, in the few random thoughts that he has given, or will give, Tom, time is disappearing, into the void, of memory, that's nice, the void of memory, now, well, now, now he stands, he looks out the window at the fields dropping off to the brilliant shard that is a river, it turns out to be the Connecticut River, remarkable, he expected the traffic, far below, its muted sounds, but there are the trees and the shrubs, yet, yet they are green, odd, strange, he reserves, this time, uncanny, wait and see, wait and see, he sees a girl in a field, somewhere out there, in the midst of nature, and so on, she is in tweeds, she isn't Sheila, she can't be Janet, safe in Tom's head, he has no idea who she is,

no idea who she is, he lays his pen down, or he will, or he thinks, of that moment, when he will, how brilliantly weary this scene of comple- tion, when he may, or will, hold it, loosely, gazing, abstracted, at whatever, he may decide to place it on the desk, actually, that will have to do, actually, a table, or he may put it, behind his ear, or in his mouth, when he will pick up the photograph, from the desk, the table, Durga is revealed, or exposed, there she is, as always, she glares at him, blankly, as always, blankly, as always, Sheila, or the other girl, of whom he has, or had, no knowledge, amid the green, she who is now, not then, not imagined, she may as well be Sheila, he'll be done with it, she is, whoever she is, Sheila, she sits on a rock, the rock, the train passes, still, perhaps it is another train, chronology is all, how placid she seems, although, or perhaps because, her eyes are blank, they are like the eyes of, of something, of someone, her expression is oddly, strangely, lascivious, defiantly so, she reminds someone on the train, perhaps Fred, perhaps Tom, there they are, in the window, or windows, of someone outside the train, someone once seen, or well known, someone that they, and he, would like to remember, or pretend to remember,

pretend to remember, everything is still, a reasonable way to pretend to end things, he will dispense with the fly, the clock, the breathing, the buzzing, ticking, sound of his own, he realizes that it is growing darker, and, right, colder, now, so to speak, now, it is completely dark, he thinks to save time, dark, dark, but now, he can't find the photograph, he looks out the window, the girl who was not Sheila, is not Sheila, is walking toward him, it is still light, outside the window, he hadn't thought of that, the swing of her hips, the way her skirt caresses her thighs, these awaken in him thoughts of etcetera, she stops, she certainly looks like Sheila, she is cognizant of being watched, she knows her role perfectly, she raises her skirt, demurely, she refastens one of her stockings, her legs, or the one leg that he can see, are, it, it is beautiful, he moves closer to the window, he has no idea who she is, he can see the lace edge of her white slip, now she shakes her skirt down, smooths it over her hips, her thighs, she looks something like his invented wife, who used to be somebody, some character, some word, in a tale, written, or told, written is better, perhaps the word was Janet, or Sheila, Sheila sounds right, as he stares she disappears, well, she doesn't disappear, she walks away, he has her walk away, he is not a voyeur, not in this tale, not now, not outside, whatever that means, not outside the photograph, which he may well have taken, which he might as well have taken, he turns to the desk, actually the table, actually will have to do, hesitant, that's precise enough, hesitant, he can't, as he feared, find the photograph, the scene, the scene that he has decided to, decided to what?, he turns on the lamp, a lamp, all right, it is the only lamp, the lamp, Durga, the figurine of Durga, glares at him, not at him, nor does she glare, there she, there it is, a dull brass figurine, he still cannot find the photograph, it is, it seems, nowhere to be found, nowhere in the room, not on the desk, the table, in any event, the room can wait, he hadn't thought of a room anyway, it is definitely missing, yet he had, and quite recently, a part, or parts, of certain elements depicted in it, yet it is missing, it may be lost, at least for now, he says aloud, and again, for now, but it is not, not really, really will have to do, he will write, but it is not lost.

Bedsteade

They say that nobody knows and nobody seems to care that April is a drunk now, lying in bed all day long. The moments pass into hours, the television soundlessly flickering before her in the best tradition of the exhausted motif, a glass of vodka at her side, some say at her elbow, thinking of her youth, her marriage, her career, whatever it was, all now dissolved in alcohol, that's what they say. She ain't got nobody. They say that such a portrait of her is a romantic lie, that she is the same old April and that Vermont has become her true home, that it reminds her of Schenectady. They say she's smilin' through. They say that Dick writes all day long in a small outbuilding that has been converted into a studio according to plans presented to the contractor by April, who has always had an eye for such detail, a flourish, a flair, a touch of elegance and style. So they say. They say no, it isn't so, that Dick is gone, that he's now just a vagabond lover. They say that April divorced Dick when she discovered him and their neighbor's wife in, as they say, vile embrace on the kitchen table, love will find a way, one fine bright morning in early spring. They say that they remarked that everything was peaches. They say that April got that wonderful look in her eye and became a nun, seized, as she was, by this perfect image of renunciation and penitence, and influenced, in no small part, by the role played so perfectly by Rose Zeppole in *Madame Delbène*. Rose, or so they say, is sometimes called Broadway Rose. They say that there's a broken heart for every light on Broadway and that Rose's is one of them. But, they say, if April did indeed become a nun how is it that this was not reported? Many say that she's just a girl that men forget. Some say that it has been reported, but in metonymic terms, for instance, that it happened in Monterey, although others say that the terms were heavily symbolic, that, in a way, the dawn was breaking. They say that whatever may be true, nothing can satisfactorily explain what they call

100

the missing years. They say that April said that it was fascination, or that the bells were ringing, or that she found the end of the rainbow. They say that she seduced office boys and truck drivers in a sentimental attempt to regain the carefree, or salad days of her young womanhood. They say that she said that the best things in life are free. They say that Dick is dead, or that Dick has married the neighbor's wife after buying off her husband, a pig farmer, they say, of some local reputation as a good driver. Now, they say, he's lonesome and sorry. They say that Dick strolls around and around the house, his shoes crunching on the gravel, while his new wife tidies the kitchen. They say that Dick said that her eyes are blue as skies are. They say that she nervously anticipates, while tidying, April's weekly visits, although some say that April lies in bed all day, and that she's *nobody's* sweetheart now. They say that the three of them compose a Platonic ménage-à-trois of a decidedly literary cast, whatever they may mean by that, although some say that they're writing songs of love and others that they are collaborating on a novel with the working title of *Doubles Cross.* Dick said, they say, that he's sitting on top of the world. They say that Dick's new wife's contribution to the novel is the idea that a smile will go a long long way. They say that April is a drunk and cannot help phoning Dick's new wife, who, they say, she calls Karen, in the middle of the night. They say she's funny that way. They say that these calls often ruin Karen's strange gelatin desserts, why, they don't say. She may be weary. They say that April knows that Antonia Harley was crippled, years ago, by her husband, although some say that her crippling was an accident and had something to do with pigs. Others that her crippling was linked with Anton's, her husband's, outstanding collection of softball bats, one of them being employed as a weapon after Antonia had made a vegetable casserole fit, so they say that Anton said, for the pigs. They say he said other things as well. They say that Anton said that Antonia said that he was the pig it was fit for. He said that she said, they say, that she'd sooner go to bed with a bottle of vodka than with him. Others say that this wasn't possible since she had left Anton long before his interest in collecting had blossomed. They also say that Antonia despised vegetables, but that April said in her testimony that she loved them in order to make Anton look bad to the jurors. They say that April said that he took advantage of her. They say, however, that the jurors were bribed to bring in a verdict of not guilty, and that they said that his sin was loving her. Others say that the case was about two other people who lived on an adjacent farm, the people who cut down the old pine tree. But they say that there was no farm, nor, for that matter, pine tree, ever involved in any way with April's life and vice versa. Only God can make a tree, so they say. Yet they say that April and Dick never said that there was a farm, and, as a matter of fact, agree that April's house and grounds in Vermont cannot be called a farm. They say that April and Dick got the money to put down on what may or may not be a farm by organizing unsavory weekend parties for the friends of a certain Mr. Pungoe, who, they say, was at the center of a rather sinister cabal having to do with art or something that vaguely resembled it, although others say that it did not resemble it at all but was merely some kind of mess called art. They say that Pungoe was in the construction business, or the real-estate business, and that despite his clubfoot, he's got rhythm. April often thought of him, they say, in her drunkenness, and of how she had always rather liked him, despite his affliction. They say that Pungoe's affliction was unspeakable, that he'll haunt you night and day. They say that Dick, just before he left for a week in Paris with Karen, said Pungoe wore the startling blue suit that was, as they say, his trademark, in order to take people's minds off his affliction, unspeakable as it was. They say that Pungoe was Chinese, born to a restaurateur in Wichita Falls, and that he said as much, they say, to April one night when she accompanied him to an opening of Annie Flammard's at the Gom Gallery. That was the evening that Annie confessed, they say, that she's the daughter of Mother Machree, the famous madam. They say that April will tell all in her memoirs, which she works on in bed during her lucid intervals, and that she revealed, they say, that the memoirs' title will be *Strange Coincidences*. Some say that the book will be an exhaustive compilation of strange coincidences. They say that Karen said that April said, although this was some time before April knew what was going on between Karen and Dick, that one of the coincidences had to do with the fact that her bed was once owned by a woman who had not only lived in Schenectady but who had known her father for many years. He used to love her but it's all over now. Karen said that April said that the woman's husband, from whom she had bought the bed, had said small world, and that he went on to say that that was what his wife would have said, rest her soul, were she still with us. April said, Karen said, that by us the emaciated widower clearly meant those of us who are still alive. Or perhaps those of us who were alive at the time of purchase. Or those of us who still are or were mostly sane. They say that April's sister, May, was the girl that Dick really wanted to marry, and that he had carried a torch, as they say, for her for years. She'll always be the same sweet girl. They say that although May didn't say that this had been the case, she didn't dismiss the notion either. She didn't say yes and she didn't say no. They say that May had at one time entertained a profound obsession concerning one of the priests at Our Lady of the Bleeding Eyes in Mechanicville, that he had brought a new kind of love to her, and that she, for a time, seriously considered taking the veil. Some say that this is a complete distortion of the facts, since it was, they say, April who thought of becoming a nun after she discovered Dick's head between Karen's thighs one fine bright morning in early spring. Her heart stood still. They say that there is nothing quite like spring in Vermont, unless, of course, one takes the moonlight into account. The moonlight, they say, is not only beautiful, some even say stunning, but is also famous. The stars at night are big and bright as well. They say that May married, finally, a nice young man, Michael Cullinan, or Cullinane, although it turned out that Mike, as they say that May said that he said he preferred to be called, was not what might be called thoroughly normal. They also say that he's not much on looks. They say that Mike and May and their two children, Brian and Maureen, visited April and Dick in Vermont one weekend after they had made the old farmhouse more or less livable, although some say that it was not a farmhouse at all. Karen said that Dick said, after they were settled in their seats in the jet that was taking them to the Bahamas for a break from the endless New England winter, that April said that she had walked in on Mike in the guest bedroom on the second day of their visit and was embarrassed by the sight that greeted her. She said, so Karen said that Dick said, that she refused to tell Dick about it, since, as they say, Dick despised both Mike and May, even though Dick and May had once been engaged while they were all at Mechanicville High together. The thrill is gone. But Antonia, who got to know April fairly well, and who, they say, even worked for a time as her amanuensis, said, or so Lena Schmidt said, or wrote, that April tells the story of "Mike in the Morning," as she calls the episode, in *Doubles Cross,* and some say that it found its way into *Strange Coincidences* as well. Although neither book has been published, nor completed, nor, some say, begun, Crescent and Chattaway seems to be interested in one or both of them. At C and C, or so they say, anything goes! Antonia said, so Lena said, or wrote, that April said that when she walked into the bedroom on that fine bright morning in early spring, she discovered Mike lying naked and supine on the bed, a pair of what April recognized as her panties wrapped around his erect penis and what she thought was one of her brassieres in his teeth, and that Mike was vigorously, as they say, abusing himself. Antonia said that Lena said, or wrote, that April said that Mike, when discovered, said, "Happy days are here again." They say that May never found out about this bizarre episode in her husband's life, although Lena said, or wrote, so Antonia said, that May must have known of Mike's sexual proclivities, even though he was a devout Catholic, as they say, a member of the Knights of Columbus in Schenectady, and deeply in favor of life. They say that he loves a parade. April, they say, threw that particular bed out or put it up for sale, or insisted that Dick put the bed in the outbuilding that was soon to be the studio in which he would engage in various literary pursuits. But others say that she sold the bed to an old friend of her father's in Schenectady. They say that April never quite got over that scene and that when she went back to work she became as promiscuous as she had been before meeting Dick at the Dew Drop Inn, a local tavern. Love is the best of all, so what the hell. Yet they say that Mike said, or that Dick said that Mike said, one night when the moon was all aglow and they had been drinking for some hours, that all the stories about April were untrue, and that May had said that Dick himself had made up all the stories about April since Dick, so Dick said Mike said May said, was angry with April since he had been jilted by May. They say that Dick laughed at Mike and made a crude and highly offensive double entendre concerning May's forever disappearing underwear. Mike had stumbled out, crying, into the bitter cold Schenectady night, although some say that this incident occurred in Vermont while April was in bed drunk, as usual. Dick says, they say, that he's sorry that he made him cry. Some say that Mike froze to death and that Lena Schmidt and Biff Page found him in the drifts, clutching a rosary. Biff says that Mike said that somebody stole his girl, then quietly expired. They say that May didn't shed a tear at his funeral. It was the talk of the town. They say that April, however, cried uncontrollably, leaning for support on Rose Zeppole's shoulder, who, they say, was dressed as a nun. They say that Rose often affected such garb, even though she was not a nun, and Léonie Aubois said that she was not only not a nun, but that her name was actually Sylvie Lacruseille, although April said that Rose says that she's often called Rose of Washington Square, although she has no idea why. All this, they say, proves that April was never a nun either, for at this time she had taken to her bed, as they say, with a bottle of vodka, the television flickering soundlessly before her, the images bringing to her mind her lost youth. Time hurries by. They say that Karen left Dick on the beach in the Bahamas for a young entrepreneur, who, they say, was just a gigolo. Dick, they say, is still on the beach, waiting patiently for her return with the cigarettes that Karen said that she wanted to buy. Others say that this is but a bad as well as ancient joke. Antonia, before she lost the power of speech in the mysterious accident which befell her, said that the whole story was suspect, since she knew, she said, that *Doubles Cross* contains a scene in which these events occur, in an episode entitled "Butts on the Beach," but others say that they've heard from people who've read the manuscript that no such scene therein exists. Others say that there is no manuscript. They say that April is the same old April and that it would be exactly like her to throw that episode away in order to protect Dick from, as she said, scorn and contumely. She can't help loving that man. They say that she sits in bed all day, drinking vodka and writing long love letters to him, and that she encloses, with these letters, erotically posed photographs of herself in various stages of undress, photographs that, they say, were taken twenty-five years ago, when, they say, she had a "blue room," which phrase no one seems able or willing to elucidate. Then, or so they say, April mails, or has mailed, these letters to Dick's new wife, Karen, who never receives them, since she has been dead for ten years, and Dick, they say, lives somewhere in New Jersey. Sometimes he's happy. They say that the Postmaster has all the letters and that he has been considering paying April a visit for some time since, they say, he doesn't realize that the young and beautiful woman wantonly posed for her husband's pleasure is the demented and drunken woman to whom he delivers mail, most of it, so they say, junk mail and bills. They say that he says that he sees her in his dreams. They say that nobody will tell him the truth about April, although others say that nobody *can* tell him the truth, for nobody knows that he possesses the letters and photographs. They say that April is getting "stranger," since she often speaks of the Postmaster with affection, although they say that what she says about him reveals that she thinks of him as he was some twenty-five years ago, when he was young and perverse, rather than as he is now, old and still perverse. They say he can dance with everybody but his wife. They say that Lena said, or wrote, that she has gone back to Mother Church because, or so Lena said, or wrote, that April said, she envies the camaraderie that exists among a group of housewives in the parish, all of them April's age, who take turns going to each other's houses for coffee and cake on weekday evenings following Benediction. These women say that there are smiles that make you happy. They say that either Lena or April is lying, since there are no housewives in the vicinity, unless, they say, Dick's new wife, Karen, may be considered such, although she is not middle-aged but quite young. They say that Karen is always chasing rainbows and that she calls herself Karen at Dick's request, even though her true name is Rose Marie. Saul Blanche, an erstwhile neighbor of the Detectives in Connecticut, said that Marcella Butler, who assisted him in a small publishing venture he had once run and who knew Dick and April when they first arrived in New York from Schenectady, Dick all pimples and April thin as a rail, said that Dick, for some unknown yet decidedly eccentric reason, fell in love with any woman named Karen, except, so they say that Saul said that Marcella said, when he fell in love with women who were not named Karen. In the latter cases, he implored these women to permit him to call them Karen. Yet some say that Marcella lied about this as she has always lied about everything concerning Dick. He is, they say, the cream in her coffee, and reminds her of her first flame, an elderly and distinguished reinsurance clerk named Fred, of whom, as they say, nothing will be said, except that at present the girl in his arms isn't she. They say that this is a blessing for Marcella, and that old Fred will miss the sweetest girl he ever had. They say that April calls Dick's new wife, Karen, Miss Dubuque, although no one can guess why, and Dick says that Karen, who is the youngest daughter of Rosie O'Grady, says that she is getting tired of being confused with some French whore whom Dick had known before they met. They say that Dick knew a number of French whores before he met his new wife, Karen, but that none of them were called Miss Dubuque, although one of them was called, oddly enough, Karen O'Grady. However, they say that the Postmaster made this story up so that he might have an excuse to call on April and warn her to stop harassing Karen, since one of the duties of the Postmaster in the little Vermont town in which all these people live is to act as the Constable. They say that the Postmaster-Constable did, indeed, visit April one night, or so he said, and that he discovered her in bed with a bottle of vodka and a man with a movie camera and an unspeakable affliction. The latter, so the Postmaster-Constable said, cheerfully introduced himself as Mr. Harlan and April as Miss Majorska, and then suggested that a threesome might be amusing since the night was made for love. They say that the Postmaster-Constable, whose name, or so he said, was Clive Oak, said that he'd come to make known to April a citizen's complaint, not to indulge in what Oak said that Harlan said were carefree gambols. But some say that none of Oak's recollections of that night rings true since he is known throughout the county as a man who would, as they say, fuck a snake. Oak, when so accused, simply says that he wants to be *happy*. They say that Oak would most certainly have joined the couple in bed, despite the fact that Harlan's affliction, unspeakable as it was, would have disgusted any reasonable human being and that Harlan's facetious remark, "You ought to be in pictures," would, most likely, have been the thing that served to convince him to join in, as they say, the fun. It is said that they say that it was after this particular adventure that April took the veil and became Sister Rocco Portola, which was the name, or so an unnamed cleaning woman said, of the nun who had given April her first catechism instruction when she was a pupil at O.L.B.E. Parochial School. But another unnamed cleaning woman said that the nun's name was Sister San Antonio Rose. In any event, as far as April is concerned, so she says, she's to this day the one rose that's left in her heart. They say that all this was a lie made up by Dick to explain April's absence from Vermont, although Karen said that Dick said that April was never absent from Vermont, and that April's memoirs clearly state that she had not left Vermont at that time, since the vodka as well as Mr. Harlan barely allowed her a moment out of bed. Those who have had the privilege of perusing April's memoirs say that they note that Oak got Mr. Harlan's name wrong, and that the man who was in bed with April was, in fact, Mr. Pungoe. The memoirs go on to say that he "does something" to her. But, they say, none of this can be trusted, for the pages of the memoirs on which these elements appear are decisively marked FOR NOVEL ONLY, the novel being, of course, *Doubles Cross,* the variant title for which was, at one time, *There's a New Sun in the Sky.* They say that Marcella said that Sheila Henry said that the first, preferred title of this novel, which title has never been revealed, although no one seems to know why, is a pun that refers to the dress, a sleeveless shift of off-white raw silk, worn by May on the evening that Mike first took her out. They say that May said that the stars were peekabooing down and that they went dancing at Lena's Rest, where Mike played "I Can Dream, Can't I?" twenty-six times on the jukebox. They say that May said that Mike proposed to her that very night, bewitched by her daring dress. They say that falling in love is wonderful. They say that Mike says that he still wonders what would have happened had May worn her pink jersey sleeveless dress, a garment, so Mike says, that could not fascinate or excite anyone but a hermit, although some say that Mike would never have used the word fascinate. On hearing this obvious denigration of his linguistic skills, Mike said that none of these insults faze him since he always lets a smile be his umbrella. He'll get by. They say that May's story is highly suspect, since April said that May said that *she* proposed to Mike. They had been high-school sweethearts, as they say, and Dick said that Mike once said that they had invariably obeyed the injunctions, or at least the suggestions, of the lyrics of certain popular songs. These lyrics had led, inevitably, to the proposal, although Dick said that Mike said nothing about who had proposed to whom. Mike also said, with a tear in his eye, that May, or for that matter, any pretty girl is like a melody that haunts you night and day, much to Dick's barely contained amusement. But they say that May never once mentioned her earlier involvement with Dick to Mike, even though April said that Dick said, years later while they were sitting in front of the fire in Connecticut, that he and May had had some great times together in the balcony of the Ritz movie theater, the Score Motor Inn, and the backseat of an abandoned Nash down by the lumber yard, and that May had been sweet and hot. They say that Mike and May were married against his parents' wishes, for, they say, the elder Cullinans or Cullinanes maintained that May was no better than her tramp of a sister, although Sister Rocco Portola, or, as some called her, Rose, said that April, at the time, was far from being a tramp and was thinking seriously of becoming a novice with the Sisters of Misericordia, a charitable order. But some say that this recollection was really no more than love sending a little gift of Rose's. Sister Rocco also said, however, that there's a little bit of bad in every good little girl, and that April had been no exception. They say that April said that May brought all this up to her one evening during a visit to the Detectives by Mike, May, Brian, and Maureen, although Maureen said, some years later, that her mother had said nothing about any of these things. But Mike says, or so Dick says that he said, that nothing that Maureen said, ever, could be trusted, since she was born to make trouble for him and May. She ain't nobody's darling. They say that it got back to April that Mike also said that Maureen took after her aunt, whom Mike dismissed as no better than a secondhand rose, and that it was clear to April that Mike had not intended to flatter her with this remark, since he made it, so Lena said, or wrote, immediately following a disturbing incident involving his daughter. They say that Mike said, so Lena said, or wrote, that he had come upon Maureen in their basement family room one evening after he and May had unexpectedly returned from a party early, a party that had been the occasion for a quarrel stemming from May's sudden and startling declaration of her unutterable boredom with his unutterably boring friends. They say that Mike's friends may well have been unutterably boring in that they spoke of little save automotive problems, trips to Europe, money, and professional football, although others say that these "subjects" are fraught with interest. In any event, Lena said, or wrote, that Mike said that he had found Maureen, who was sixteen at the time, rather intimately involved with two neighborhood boys of her own age, and that their partially undressed state was explained to him by his daughter as the result of a game of charades. They say that April said that when she heard, or read, what Lena said, or wrote, about what Mike had said that Maureen had said that Mike should have been glad that *somebody* loves her. They also say that when it got back to April that Mike had compared Maureen to her aunt, the "tramp," and that the comparison had been based, doubtlessly, on the incident in the family room, she had suggested that she might ask May to ask Mike about what she said was the little faux pas of some few years earlier concerning certain articles of intimate feminine apparel. Every road has a turning. They say that somebody told this to Mike and that he became so upset that he left the house in the middle of a professional football game. But others say that nothing short of death or a sale of repp-stripe ties could make Mike miss a professional football game, and, as a matter of fact, that Mike's abiding dislike of Sheila Henry was rooted in the fact that she had once asked Mike if it were really true that all football players are homosexuals. They say that April said that she hoped Mike would suffer a fatal coronary just before the kickoff of the next Super Bowl game. They say that Mike did indeed suffer such an attack, but others disagree, and say that he had a spontaneous orgasm. They say that *Karen* was the one who suffered a fatal coronary, and that soon after Dick met another young woman, whose name was Karen. They say that this Karen was an airline hostess and that April said that Dick said to all who would listen that this Karen was "*the* one," and that he'd found a rose in the devil's garden, whatever he meant by that. April said, or so Marcella said that Dick said, that she was certain that this Karen's surname was Minet, another "healthy slut," and that Dick said that this was but another of April's drunken insults and that he was sorry that he'd left the Vermont house to her. Marcella said that April laughed at this and noted merely that the sun was going to shine in her back door some day. Marcella said that Dick had begun to cry and told her that the Vermont house was where he had first discovered that his true bent was for literary pursuits. But they say that Dick never wrote anything anywhere, and that the novel *Blackjack,* which he claimed as his own, had been written by Henri Kink, who, so they say, disappeared some years ago. Days are long since he went away. Henri had had an argument with Annette Lorpailleur, who, so they say Madame Delamode said, had been secretly married to Mr. Pungoe for some time. But Joanne Lewis said that Annette and Pungoe had never been married, although they say that Joanne cannot be trusted in anything that she says ever since the day that she moved in with a man named Norman, whom, they say, nobody has ever laid eyes on with the exception of Joanne and her ex-husband, Guy, who *still* gets jealous. Yet they say that Guy cannot be trusted in anything that *he* says concerning Joanne. He has, as they say, gone around the bend, and spends his nights all alone by the telephone, waiting for some mysterious call that will prove to the whole world that you're a million miles from nowhere when you're one little mile from home. Joanne, they say, doesn't believe a word of this. When April heard of Joanne's new relationship, they say that she stopped drinking and became engaged to Oak, who, so Karen, Dick's new wife, not Karen Minet, said. She went on to say that Oak said to her that this was a dream come true, that he'd found a million-dollar baby. They say that Oak has never got over the twenty-five-year-old photographs of April that he still cherishes. Some say that the joke, if joke it was, was on Oak, as, twenty-five years earlier, it had been on Dick, in that the photographs were not, so Mike said that May said, of April at all, but of her, May. April says that this is nonsense, as does Dick, but May said, so Mike says, that it is the absolute truth, since she and April are identical twins. She even says that an old family saying has it that April brings the flowers that bloom in May. So much, as they say, for old family sayings. But they say that this contention is absurd, since April and May do not look at all alike, although others say that they can't be told apart. Mike says that May insisted that this was the fact, and that she had said this one day when she was, so Mike says May said, "up to here" catering to the whims of his drunken family, members of which would, so they say, descend upon Mike and May at all hours. They say that Marcella said that April said that Mike said that what had made him furious, even though he still loved May as he had loved her when she was sweet sixteen, was that May had asked his father if he didn't feel cold without his green cardboard derby. But others say that May's language was more forceful and that she had said to the elder Cullinan or Cullinane that he looked blue without his fucking shanty green fucking derby. Yet May said, so April says, that she would never have used such language in front of Brian, who was, at the time, an altar boy at O.L.B.E. They say that April, despite her engagement to Oak, or perhaps because of it, began drinking again, that Oak finally joined her, and that the two of them spend their days and nights watching television. Yet Karen, Dick's second ex-wife, said that Oak said, on one of his daily visits to her in the new condominium development where she lives, that it is April who drinks and watches television, and that he, so Karen said he said, had moved into Dick's old studio, where he spends his time in research on the writings of Anatole Broyard. Oak says, they say, that his feverish labors are worth all his sacrifices, because the world is *waiting* for the sunrise. Some say that Norman, for some reason, bought the condominium for Karen, but others say that Norman has never heard of Karen. For her part, Karen says that the condominium was a gift from Barnett Tete, who admires, so Karen says, New England spunk. Karen and April, they say, have returned to Mother Church, and like nothing better than to chat, over coffee and cake, with the other women of the parish on weeknights following Benediction. They say that April says that she has burned her memoirs, despite Crescent and Chattaway's interest, and that she has recently taken to telephoning May in order to dissuade her from the sin of divorcing Mike, who, so Karen says that April said that May said, has begun to take what she called a "morbid" interest in her wardrobe. Mike speaks to April, they say, after she has spoken to May and begs her not to reveal to her a certain secret that they share, a secret, so May says that Mike said, that has to do with a practical joke that he played on April some years ago on a fine bright morning in early spring, or, as he says in what he calls "play-talk," on the morning that he was with her in apple-blossom time. April, they say, pretends not to know what Mike means, while Karen, or so she said, to whom April has told the story of that morning, makes faces at April so that she can hardly keep from laughing while on the telephone. They say that April still despises May and that she urges her sister not to divorce Mike so that they may continue to live together as usual. But others say that April really cares for her sister, and that she truly hopes that one day she'll find her lovable. Dick, for one, believes this, they say. He has, others say, just moved into a house down the road from April and Karen with his fifth wife, Karen, who is a color consultant and loves to do pastel miniatures which she frames herself. Or so they say that April said, although Karen says April is a drunk now and never says anything at all.

Chyme of belles

There's no rush. There's never any rush, the truth, the facts, are all here, they do not have to be hurried into prominence. Serenely, they'll assert themselves, we'll get a few things straight, finally, although why it should so turn out that Anne and Ellen will have their lives rectified is beyond comprehension. The impression was that their lives had been rectified, which goes to prove how little we know. Consider the dozens of other people who must bear the burden of distortion, who have been presented as so many instances of a sketchy and unsatisfactory Eleatics, and then, of course, there is the flatness of the narrative, the lack of tension, the absence of conflict and resolution, the dying falls, the lack of closure. Coarse sexuality. Data and cynical commentary. Nervous and demotic language. Jokes! Yet all is true, each and every line. In vain we search for immense darkness, wandering gazes, garish colors, sullen heat, swooping sea gulls. And not to forget the backless kitchen chair! The leaky toilet! And the reassuring smile. *This* must be the void, deemed fashionable by those who dabble in ontology. Dare we whisper: fuck them? The stuffy room: check. The moths bumbling at the windowpane: check. Numbing somnolence of the heat that spreads over the town like a, like a: check. A screen door, right on cue, slams in the distance: check again. Here, in the silence, broken only by the scratching of a pen on paper, the buzzing of a fly breaks the silence. Wait. The stifling silence is broken by *two* sounds, the scratching of a pen on paper and the buzzing of a fly. Face to face with the unbearable light of truth!

Anne

Her maiden name was not Marshall, but McCoyne. Scratch the telephone company. Anne couldn't catch a ball for the life of her, nor run,

nor wrestle. The radio. All right. The radio is what she liked! The other
members of the Christian Conservative Student Crusade disapproved
of her and her clothes, especially her flour-smudged skirts. Her hair was
dark brown, she wrote home to her mother, Charlotte Pugh McCoy,
McCoyne, every week. An occasional gravy stain. Charlotte, too,
listened to the radio, driving her husband, in desperation, to the
Bluebird Inn, where he learned how to do a passable fox-trot. What the
hell, it filled his empty life with promise, his empty and somnolent life.
This dance may figure large in our story, like a symbol, of which we
have a plethora. Transcendence is all. Anne always wore underclothes,
even, strangely, beneath her bathing suit, for she adored swimming. On
almost any summer Sunday, she could be found at Riis Park, her face
dreamy as she listened to one of her many radios. Her preference was
for white rayon, which is fine by me. Pristine. There were few problems
that she couldn't solve, once she undid her braids. She did not know
how to throw pots or make, let's say make, ceramics, and as for knitting,
crocheting, and sewing, they, she often said, her eyes snapping with the
irrepressible humor that, her eyes glowing with girlish fun, they, well,
were for other people. That's how she put it. Sometimes she wore a
single braid. Thick, of course. Tania Crosse, her first roommate, loved
it when she claimed, as she barely repressed a shy giggle, that she could
weave. A grotesque ashtray had somehow found its way into the
apartment. Actually, Tania was her second roommate. Anne often
gazed imperturbably at it, wondering if the unbearable heat would ever
break. She had no curtains. Sun is sun, but *this!* One evening, she and
Tania experimented together sexually, and though nothing came of it,
Anne's heart pounded when she thought, in later years, of Tania's
creamy skin and soft lips. Her pulses crooned. Yielding and such. She
never married Guy Lewis, nor even met him until long after her
marriage to Leo. That clears that up. Her blood seemed to boil, too.
Olga Begone? An invention. We already know about the nonexistent
Tessie and Jude. Charlotte sent her a set of chili bowls, suitable, of
course, for soup or stew as well. Or even salad. Anne occasionally
made soup or stew, but chili, never. Most of the time she was content to
know that the bowls sat neatly in the cupboard, a token of her old life.
Oddly enough, she had, some years before, confessed her loathing of
certain hearty dishes to Ralph Ingeman, an old school friend, or chum.

Ralph's open face had broken into an engaging grin when he heard this news. He, for his part, was not surprised, for he had always been a salad fan. Ralph still wrote to her, his letters invariably beginning with the salutation, "Dear New York Pal," which phrase occasionally made Anne retch. Yet more often than not she'd sit, alone at the kitchen table, or she'd sit alone, at the kitchen counter, after reading Ralph's chatty letters, and allow nostalgia to wash over her like an invisible wave of sullen heat. Enough? More.

Ellen

Jackie Moline never existed, one can check with Ellen on that. Her salad was reasonably good, the ingredients were fresh, although she had a penchant for bottled dressing, especially a remarkably tasty concoction called Green Goddess. Perhaps it was a sign. Strange how salad has popped up again. She often capped the bottle with an unsteady hand, sweat forming in little beads on her worried brow. She wore a cocktail dress but once, to her high-school prom, and it made her feel, well, beautiful. As well it should have. Photographs from those days reveal her slender waist and large breasts, but a discreet device planted in her ear hints at early hearing problems. So there is a measure of heartache to be taken into account. Wearing this dress, she longed to turn away from her callow classmates and their little dreams. Peck and Peck? Fabrication. But after the dance, alone in her stuffy room, the house gripped by the unseasonably hot June night, she was grudgingly forced to admit that some of them had big dreams. She met Leo long after he and Anne had been divorced, and could never forget how the blood had thudded in her temples when she first saw him, his great artistic head of hair setting him apart from the crowd, which was quite large. She was a graduate of Brooklyn College, and although she had, indeed, a pert snub nose, this latter was the result of what her mother irritatingly called a nose job. Elizabeth Reese was a philosophy teaching assistant, a young woman with bow legs and a sudden but warm smile. The operation had cost, as her father often put it, "plenty." She was properly thankful. Big tits aren't everything, as Mother Theresa probably knows. When Ellen looked at Elizabeth she felt suddenly faint, as if the blood beneath her tingling flesh had grown wildly turgid. At such times, she sensed her woman's body keenly, and a strange excitement made her catch her breath. But school ended, and goodbye Miss Reese! One hot summer day, a day on which the cruel and scorching air hung, then fell over the city like a leaden blanket, she got a job. She was glad when the shadows finally lengthened for she could hardly wait to enter the candy store around the corner from her parents' house. It would be good, she thought, the faint trace of a smile playing across her full mouth, to relax and have an egg cream and an Eskimo Pie at the counter. For it must be understood that Ellen, despite the harsh disappointments of her childhood, had few, if any, problems with acne. She was lucky, "glad" is how she thought of it, to have landed the job. It was time for her to sever her ties with Jake, her father, and Tessie, her mother, whose existence centered on her weekly Mah-Jongg game. Jake, for his part, liked nothing better than a good cigar. The clicking of the tiles and the voices of her mother's friends always made her think of the overpowering bouquet of her father's cheap cigars, and the gestalt of these invariables caused her to shudder imperceptibly. She would turn away, grimacing, her heart heavy with the nagging sense of her betrayal of them. At such moments, Jake would whisper encouragement to her, secure in the knowledge that she couldn't hear him. She would often remain sleepless throughout the long nights, rising at dawn to watch the salmon-pink sky spread its glory over the world. Her large, youthful breasts trembled beneath her sheer nightgown, and suddenly there would appear against the vast sunrise a gull, serene in the sky, proud and isolate. Her nipples often rose against the diaphanous fabric. Enough? More.

Anne

It wasn't Theodore Roethke who mattered, but Peter Viereck, or perhaps Allen Tate, in any event, one of our great poets. She loved those poems, strong as they were, yet with a certain delicacy and a rapt attention to rational form. And the fact that they meant something, that they transcended and explained many things didn't hurt either. "The Old Confederate Dead Man" was, perhaps, her favorite. Craig Garf took it into his grizzled head to hump her quietly at a party one evening, and she, stricken with nameless grief and half-mad with strong drink and the passionate rhythms of loud music, probably hot jazz, humped him frenziedly back. She never lived in Brooklyn, that mysterious borough as foreign to her as the mysterious Bronx. Leo came into her life at about the same time that the strange ashtray appeared, on a cold day when the grey sky seemed to complement her depressed spirits. It loured menacingly. What a head of hair! she thought shyly. He sent her a drink at a bar that everyone frequented, including the *Lorzu* crowd, and when she asked him his name he smiled distantly, and, in reply, bit off a few obscure words. They hung in the air for a long moment and time, at least as far as she was concerned, seemed to stop. Then she knew, she felt him somehow deeply and irrevocably hers. At about the time—it was summer now, a deadening, humid, somnolent summer whose heat lay on the city like a sweaty hand, or arm—that she found herself becoming involved with Leo, Charlotte, her mother, wrote to tell her that she was remarrying and that the groom was to be Russell Gunge, the aging barber who lived just upstairs. At the news, a bleak greyness, a greyness like that of a bleak, grey November day, settled on her soul. Not that she didn't like Russ, who smoked Pall Malls, but she couldn't help but remember his mocking leer when, as a girl, she had excitedly told him of her plans for the future. You be locky if yez loins ta fock-trot like ya dad, he'd invariably say, his scissors held menacingly aloft. On one occasion, he had gestured cynically with the yellowed fingers that now often returned to haunt her waking dreams. The diaper story is slanderous and apocryphal, or probably so, since the tastes of most of her male friends ran to lacy underwear and sheer hosiery, nothing, as they say, to write home about, at least not in a lather. Babies, and all that served to remind Leo of babies, put the unkempt poet off. He would lie on his rumpled bed, tears welling up in his eyes, a foxed copy of Wordsworth, an English poet, open on his bare chest to "The Prelude," a highly regarded poem of several parts. Soon after, they married, but Leo turned out to be, to put a nice face on it, not up to the mark, and even though Anne often thought of the beauty of the hills as they turned to gold under the evening sun, and of how wonderful Indians really were, it was all she could do to clear a space for herself amid the clutter of the dining table, or, as things might have it, the kitchen table. She smoked nervously. Enough? More.

Ellen

Yet after the family ties were severed and placed on the dumbwaiter, she felt somehow as if she were the only human being in the world, and often found herself crying as if in expectation of a curse and a blow. Her legs, which even now are a splendid eyeful, were especially lovely way back when, and it wasn't long before the hirsute bard was running his hands under her skirt while they sat in one or another of the dimly lit boîtes or cocktail lounges in which he cut something of a figure. To tell the truth, he adored playing with her garters, or, as he'd often gaily whisper in her ear, her jarretières. The night that found Leo really getting fresh with her was the turning point in their relationship, and although it had little or nothing to do with the party's baked ham, roast turkey, or cold cuts, it was a shock nonetheless to Ellen to realize that the insistent pleasure between her thighs was being caused by his somewhat importunate if pleasantly feverish hand. The French have an expression for that, she thought, somewhat irrelevantly. They left to confront a rain that poured down sullenly, like a great wet hand, on the city, a wet and cold and merciless hand, and Leo's voice rose in triumph as he turned at the door to hurl imprecations at poor Jack Towne. Ellen felt, after all this, barely alive, and wondered what Miss Reese would have thought when, later, she surrendered to Leo's pathetic lusts. Her skin felt hot beneath her woolen suit, or perhaps one of her innumerable cocktail dresses, oddly fetching garments which she had taken to wearing again, despite coarse laughter. Her skin cooled quickly as Leo undressed her with shaking hands, and she was secretly glad that the lace on her underthings was as fine and frothy as spun sugar or beaten egg whites. What a break! Then the world seemed to move away, slowly, silently, and everything in Leo's flat receded into a magical and shimmering distance. And a good thing too. She wondered, as she felt the poet's urgent manhood at the center of her yielding body, what Jackie might have said had Jackie only been, as she had often dreamily wished, her brother. But she had no brother! No, she had nothing, nothing but Jake and Tessie of whom, she thought guiltily, she was just a little ashamed, now that she had begun to meet really sophisticated people. Enough? More.

Anne

Biscayne Bay does not figure in our narrative, so that all references to it and environs should be viewed as apocryphal at best. Yet perhaps the mere notice of the words occasioned by a fleeting glance at a magazine made Leo question the wisdom of their marriage, for Anne even now recalls that it was after just such a cursory, or fleeting glance that Leo became cynical, hostile, sardonic and contemptuous toward her. Her spirits sank as if into a sea upon whose surface of hope no ship of love or even affection could move or tack in the becalmed waters that . . . sank as if they were a ship into the becalmed waters of a lost sea, a lost and strange sea, a Sargasso of crushed dreams and thwarted hopes. She introduced him to one of her new friends, Léonie Aubois, brilliant, embittered, wise-cracking Léonie, in the hope that the latter would refresh his spirits by chatting with him of the latest fashions in frillies, lacies, gewgaws, and equipment. It was to no avail. Indeed, Anne often started awake to the mad flutes and drums or fifes and drums of large orchestras or bands playing Civil War songs. Leo would often sing along, his voice raised in agonized triumph. Her haunted eyes would gaze imploringly at him over their light but nourishing Continental breakfast, and he would, rarely, all too rarely, meet them with his own imploring gaze. Yet nothing seemed amenable to resolution, although when she found a pair of ice-blue panties among Leo's papers her heart sang, for she knew that he had bought them for her as an offering to Eros, as a gesture toward their mislaid passion or, at the very least, mutually satisfying marital sex. But her spirits sank in the ponderous July heat, an oppressive heat that smothered the city like a damp muffler, when, the next day, she saw Frieda Canula, the manager of a laundromat down the street, with the intimate garment nonchalantly knotted about her neck. So much for froufrous, she thought, drained, as she dashed at the tears that sprang to her eyes and then ran, like slow, sad rivers, down her pale cheeks. The Detectives? Anne disliked them intensely, even though, at this time, she hardly knew them, and didn't want to, given the fact that she was barely alive, what with the oppressive heat's leaden hands choking the city, the ceaseless grey rain, and the gnawing sadness that ate at her like an acid regret. The presence of a packet of photographs that belie her nodding acquaintance with Dick and April should, of course, be noted, but only *en,* as the French so deftly put it, *passant, mes amis.* [But just while passing by, my pals.] Muscatel? Yes. White Port, Thunderbird, Sherry, Gypsy Rose—all these went down Leo's throat, and with each swallow he slipped deeper and deeper into his strange apathy, an apathy in which the sublime art that had always been his reason, or one of his many reasons, for living, was deeply foundering, so that Leo and Anne were both gasping in the long, relentless, hot summer with its leaden skies and fierce, hot rains, those scorching rains that, because they were hot and scorching, made the summer hotter and more relentless. Anne threw herself into bed one evening with ZuZu Jefferson, the cool and fashionable blonde who had an interesting and demanding job having something pertinent to do with, as Leo's beloved Wordsworth once put it, "creative art!" He knew what he was talking about. Never had Anne's body felt so alive! Never had the roots of her sexuality been so deeply stirred! Never had her soul so yearned to cry out, its voice high in ecstatic joy: SO THIS IS THE ORGASMIC ACTIVITY THAT I'VE BEEN READING ABOUT IN A NUMBER OF RECENT MAGAZINE ARTICLES! Wow! she cried, again and again. Wow! It was really something. She soon bought a fedora and began keeping a journal in which she recorded her most private thoughts and impressions, thoughts and impressions now safe from Leo's drunken contempt, cold hostility, bitter cynicism, mocking leer or leers, and proud contumely. Enough? More.

Ellen

Some of them were not, surely, as sophisticated as were others, for instance, there was the insufferable clubfooted man who usually went by the name of Harlan Pungoe, and who seemed to have a penchant for cameras, photographs, and what might be termed documentary evidence of this, that, and the other thing. A robust sort of tyke, no, fellow, a robust fellow who, despite his shadowy motivations, and his relentless peerings, was at bottom no more than what somebody termed a fucking cripple. However, years ago, in somebody's vague memory, it seems that Harlan was not crippled at all! Ellen tried to put it all out of her mind, yet it was always there, behind whatever other varied thoughts were hers, so that to see her stand, bemused, outside the

Foxhead Inn, in her tight bodice and short flared skirt, was to know that Pungoe had, so to speak, inserted his quite considerable self into her mental life. But even with that to worry about she had to admire her remarkable gams when she glimpsed their reflection in a passing tray. Then Barry Gatto strode into her life and she felt, momentarily, somewhat content. Perhaps it was merely the faint odor of Moo Goo Gai Pan on his breath, since he was widely respected as a gourmet. Yet whatever the temptation, Leo was never very far from her thoughts, usually just "in front," as Ellen conceived of it, those of Harlan. As far as the ex-priest, Frank Baylor, Father Frank, is concerned, he seems to have just passed through, sans stopping, the rather hectic milieu that at that time abounded. That takes care of that. There had always been something remote about him anyway, a depressing greyness, that emanated from his, so many thought, patronizing and sacrosanct attitude, if greyness can fairly be said to emanate from anything at all, much less an ex-priest's attitude. In any event, he came and went within forty-eight hours. Off to the convent! someone quipped, his indiscreet hand up Ellen's accommodatingly short skirt. They were always trying that one out on her, often with reasonably satisfying results. It goes without saying that her job as a cocktail waitress was fraught with humiliation, and at the end of her working day, as she walked out into the nearly deserted streets of the great iron uncaring city, she felt numbed, barely alive, and humiliated. In the winter, her legs would get extremely cold, especially were the winds bitter, and if it were drizzling that fine, icy, penetrant mist that brings one face to face with one's own mortality, she would find herself actually running toward the subway. It was nothing short of amazing. She'd creep up Leo's stairs as the dawn rose on the pitiless metropolis, hoping that she'd find Leo asleep as she most liked him, his arm badly twisted beneath his flamboyant aesthetic head, his cheek wet with childlike drool. Often he would be stretched out on his back and she'd take solace in the fact that the phonograph's turntable would be spinning, the needle riding in the final grooves, exactly as it does in so many of the films that Ellen had seen and, yes, loved. She wasn't ashamed to admit her liking for the cinema. He needed her then, she knew, and it was nothing for her to wake him and pose lasciviously before his fevered eyes for hours and hours, or at least for about forty-five minutes to maybe an hour or so. In the middle of

these erotic exhibitions, she'd think, Pungoe!, and rush to the dirty
window in time to see a nondescript figure in an electric-blue suit limp,
or perhaps hobble off toward a lonely diner, preferably one beneath an
"el." Eyes snapping, Leo would roughly possess her as she leaned on
the windowsill as the first rosy light appeared in the east. It was
probably her wet hosiery that excited him, wet from the cruel drizzle
that has already been mentioned. Father Frank had mentioned
something about it on the night that now loomed as one of the most
important of her life, could she only discover precisely why. Enough?
More.

Anne

A reckless artist, Tony Lamont, his gifts destroyed long years before by
an excess of critical adulation, yes, he was that. But the reality was
sadder. His rampant manhood longed to find its way to Karen's armpits
and the moist tufts of hair that he wished grew there, but it was only a
dream. Only a dream!, he would sob into the fetid air of his dank
bedroom. Anne needed the divorce from Leo and his insufferable
Dante Rossini! As far as she was concerned, a wop was, well, not to be
crude about it, always just a wop. And this despite various arias, which,
she had to admit when coaxed, took her breath away. Then there was,
finally, the discovery of the frilly items in Tony's freezer, which, when
Anne opened the door one fine spring morning, the pigeons cooing and
shitting on the window ledge, took her breath away. For a long moment,
after her breath returned whence it had fled, it came in ragged gasps and
anguished rattlings, as she recognized the frilly items, now cold as the
death of their passion, to be various intimate garments of Karen
Ostrom, who was, Anne was certain of it now, some kind of Swede. She
fairly flew down the stairs after blindly shaving her underarms, weeping
bitterly, dashing the angry tears from her eyes, those dark eyes which
snapped in irrepressible fury. Into the cloudy grey morning she ran,
quite unsure of where she was going, knowing only that she must go!
Fitful rain pelted her unmercifully, like a large and merciless fist. Lorna
Flambeaux was waiting, as usual, reclining, actually, on a heap of
pillows carelessly, yet with studied elegance, strewn about the fur rug
before the bright fire. That was Lorna all over. Anne had to admire her,

for Lorna, despite her important job and her upper-middle-class pretensions, didn't care! Then came a long, sweet morning of mutually consensual adult sexual behavior, directed toward making both of them feel good about themselves, and Anne's soul sang a long melody of rapturous sensuality, believe it or not. She, who had but a scant few hours earlier felt herself barely alive, now thrilled to the center of her being, as Lorna showed her a few perverse tricks that she'd learned from a certain "Yasmine." Yet who is to say what "perverse" is? Or who, for that matter, what "tricks" are? Her passionate laughter came so unexpectedly and powerfully that she dislodged, more than once, poor Lorna, who wound up, not unsurprisingly, utilizing the home first-aid kit before they sat down to a light and nourishing lunch, which fairly took Anne's breath away. Soon came Anne's first pair of Sweet-Orr overalls and a chance meeting with Annette Lorpailleur, who was somehow mysteriously linked with a man the crowd called "Clubfoot Pete," and who turned out to be, of course, Pungoe. Although he smiled benignly at all, and his voice was rich and deep and so bespoke more than a mediocre upbringing and education, Anne was uncomfortable with the idea of looking the other way when he commenced, as he did with great regularity, to, well, "play" with himself, a hand thrust as nonchalantly as possible, given the circumstances, into his pocket. It unfailingly took her breath away. At the funeral for Henri Kink, whose works, according to those who knew about such things, were delicate yet strong as a spiderweb, albeit filled with a joyous affirmation of life and a great humility before his responsibility to his characters, she saw Leo again. Someone insisted respectfully, as she tried not to stare, that Henri's works were as delicate and strong as a *number* of spiderwebs, not just one, for Christ's sake! She couldn't help but notice that the young woman who gazed raptly at Leo wore a cocktail dress, and she knew, suddenly, that this was Leo's future wife, Ellen Marowitz. It was a curious shade of mauve, and, to be candid, Anne thought it a little gauche. Yet the funeral ended on a dark note when a strangely importunate person with the unlikely name of Rupert Whytte-Blorenge insisted on spitting into Henri's grave and then, to add insult to injury, told Anne, to her face, that she was, as far as he was concerned, some eyeful. At this *mot* he winked and reminded her of a costume party to which she had, against her better judgment, worn a diaper and heels. So it was true. Anne blushed beet-red, backed away, then stumbled blindly, tears stinging her eyes, into the oppressive heat of the streets, the mocking laughter of the mourners pursuing her as if it would do so forever. As she stood at the curb, waiting for a taxi, and wishing fervently that she had never even heard the word "diaper," Pungoe pulled up alongside her in a new car, vulgarly shiny, his clubfoot concealed by a fetching rug, one hand insouciantly yet energetically twitching in his pocket. Ride home?, he inquired pleasantly, or, perhaps, Lift home?, and Anne got into the car, affording him a good long look at her legs. What was the use?, she thought. Pungoe crisply threw the sedan into reverse and smashed decisively into a tree. Thankfully, no real damage was done. Enough? More.

Ellen

Olga Begone, a very thin poet who had kept hidden, for some years, a novel, *Zeppelin Days,* written while a student, took a good look at Ellen one day as the latter chopped shallots and cabbage for one of her special dishes, and the brilliant if remotely obstreperous artist promptly introduced herself to the young bride. She had some legs, Olga thought. Ellen found herself strangely drawn to the warm, homely lesbian, who was, at this time of her life, a go-getter. She had more than a few things to say about the works of Robbe-Grillet! What they were, precisely, Olga could not articulate, yet this failing did nothing to prevent Ellen's disappointment when discreet inquiries revealed that the poet was currently living with Anne. It seemed unlikely, and many pals thought of Ellen's putative amazement as an affected ironic sophistication. But Ellen, like the good soldier that she was, refused to allow this letdown to affect her pursuit of other adventures, or, as she once put it, put a "crimp" in it. She was, it should be stated, chagrined at having to wear, and regularly, the famous pink jersey sleeveless dress we've heard of so often, and thought, more than once, of her empty and meaningless life. She would stare at herself in the mirror, cringing, as she listened in disgust to Leo splashing with his boats in the bathtub, readying himself, as he tenderly put it, for her. She could feel her skin crawl beneath the jersey and her eyes would grow moist, perhaps with self-pity. How she despised herself! Then the splashing would stop. The living room, into which she'd automatically walk, and which she had once been naive enough to think charming, filled her soul with a greyness that made her gorge rise. Leo would enter, his sex stirring, a Hi-Lo paddle gripped in one hand, a mocking leer disfiguring his once-sensitive features. His other hand would gesture toward the musty attic. Enough? More.

Anne

A Jackie something paid her well to perform despicable acts that made her feel degraded, almost dirty. But she made plenty of money serving these various lusts, so much so that there soon emerged a new Anne! Her face, once sensitive, now wore a perpetually mocking leer, and she offhandedly married, past hurt, past reason, Barnett Tete, a millionaire with a heart made of stone. She became known as the nun of Biscayne Bay, and was often seen wandering among the conchs. Rich and powerful people were in the area, as were golden sands. Yet wealth was not the answer to the age-old question that would form on her tight lips. It was not the answer! She returned to New York, for reasons peculiarly her own, rigid and forbidding in a tailored suit that, paradoxically, brought out the yielding femininity of her soft and still vulnerable body. She was vaguely discomfited by this, yet she had many suits. What could she do?, she mused. Throw them away? She wanted to make her life sing again. Freud had been right after all, she realized, suddenly ashamed. She appeared, for no reason at all, in a pornographic film catering to the vilest of male fantasies concerning tribadic love, as Sister Philomena Veronica, and caught the eye of Father Frank, who was back, again. He knew a great deal about ceramics and good fiction, having once been an editor at a magazine devoted to publishing really fine writing. They opened a little store together in Elmhurst, where Anne's gentle way with the clientele permitted them to reap a tidy profit. Religious stuff was their specialty and they had a batch of it. One day the vengeful shadow of Barnett Tete fell across the threshold, then the man himself followed. He had recently been released from a mental hospital, and Anne felt herself go all cold, then all hot, as she remembered certain things. A scream rose unchecked from her throat. The ceiling of the shop began to swim, sickeningly, and her knees turned to water, as, chuckling maliciously, Tete pulled from his pocket a diaper! At that moment, Father Frank entered, his eyes wide with horror. He knew. He *knew.* Enough? More.

Ellen

Despite everything, a lot had happened. Ellen thought bitterly, favoring her sore buttocks as she sat at the window table in her favorite coffee shop. There comes a time when humiliation is too high a price to pay for a few good dresses. A phrase from a great poem suddenly intruded on her half-clouded memory. If only she could remember it! She felt the breath catch in her throat. She was excited. Poems can do that, and so well, she said to herself as she paid her check. The cashier looked up quizzically, then smiled uncertainly, her eyes on Ellen as she walked out into the drizzle. Lucy! She knew now. That was what she had to do. Some days later she found herself in Lucy's homely arms, both of them thinking of the truth buried in the poem's famed lines, while Anne wept, thinking of her father—dull, inarticulate, cruel, unfeeling, just plain, well, dumb, yet the dearest man she had ever known. She thought of their little Friday ritual, which he had shyly called "gumball." "Gumball?" he'd ask softly. And she had always answered yes, yes, oh yes, Daddy! What had that been about? If only . . . Hardly any time at all passed, and one day she and Lucy found themselves on the street, arm in arm, dazed and lethargic in the afternoon heat. Leo sat on the curb, half-hidden beneath the battered fedora that Ellen recognized as a caring token given her years before by a woman who was now much older, and as she put her hand up to her mouth in the age-old womanly gesture of pity and love and sorrow, she felt somewhat odd. Lucy, ugly, faithful Lucy, said quietly, no!, and brusquely stayed Ellen from sinking to her knees before the man to whom she had once surrendered herself. "No," she repeated, since Ellen had apparently not heard her. Her hearing aid was still "on the fritz," as she'd learned to say. Better than having a clubfoot, she'd say to Pungoe, when his barbs became a little too pointed. "No!" And now, she heard. A weight seemed to slip from her shoulders. But did it? Enough? More.

Anne

Heartless mirth and objects appearing as if in a dream, exotic food products. The release of maddening desires and an end to frustration. Looking as if she hadn't a care, moving as if in a trance: harsh and liberating truth, burning and insatiable flesh. Waking dreams! Deserted hills over which the sunlight plays, pinched souls. Sudden realization of friendship. Enough? Almost.

Ellen

Sudden realization of frustration and the pinched and insatiable flesh. The release of exotic food products: heartless objects! Moving as if she hadn't a care, looking as if in a trance. Maddening desires appearing as if in a dream. An end to mirth. Burning and deserted hills and a waking friendship. Harsh sunlight, liberating souls. Dreams over which the truth plays. Enough? Enough.

Hell mought

Joanne Lewis was born in Boonton, New Jersey, a small town putatively founded by Daniel Boone in 1809. As Guy reached orgasm, she absurdly thought of Boone, but why, she could not say. Odd that she had discovered the ecstasies of art *cum* sex right there in the heart of the great uncaring city. Although the January day had been bitter cold, she and Guy had tarried long on the Provincetown sands, those silent, majestic sands of New England. How she wished that Barnard were in Massachusetts! When she saw, years later, that infernal vision on Norman's wall, diabolic above his black leather couch, it was all she could do to smile weakly at Chet Kendrick, one of the stars of *The Party,* and her escort for the evening. Barnard became, perhaps predictably, increasingly distant from her thoughts. How Norman had ever come into possession of *The Valley of the Shadow of Death* was a mystery to everyone, not least Guy. Yet she remembered Harlan's prize specimen, a ceramic dildo made in exact imitation of those that whalers were wont to carve lovingly for their wives, forlorn on the shore. The large painting, done in a somber palette, had always seemed, to her, a representation of the mouth of Hell. Harlan had said that he'd been "through hell" to find exactly what he was looking for in ceramic Pekes. Why nobody, she had suddenly thought, ever complained about oiling the adobe floors was surprising. His wonderful collection of unique ceramic ashtrays, works of art in themselves, graced many a boardroom, and had convinced her that he was indeed the salesman he purported to be. Then she whipped him again with his belt, a remarkably ornate item of tooled leather. That the point of one heart nestled in the cleft of another all around the outer circumference of the friendship ring, or so she wrote years later in her diary, "tortured her young blood" with its "innocent symbolism." Afterward, exhausted, they had looked long at the setting sun which turned the snow on the

Sangre de Cristo blood red. And Ralph had rudely taken *his* friendship ring back! The opening sentence of *Unicorn,* "The wind, which had, all the dreaming Cornish afternoon, carried intimations of a calm and joyous love, turned suddenly cruel as the sun slouched coldly into the furious sea," had stayed in her mind since she had first read it. She still had the ring, after all this time, and often thought of Stanley, who had suffered so terribly with acne. Despite her nervous exhaustion and her worry over everything, *Unicorn Crimson, Unicorn Grey* was a marvelous read. But Guy maintained that it was not the mouth of Hell there pictured, but the face of Satan himself, whom he had, he insisted, once glimpsed on a road some miles outside Kansas City. Settling once more into the pillows, she read again the flap copy for the work which "redefines, for all time, the much-abused 'historical' novel." Guy, terribly drunk, shouted that he hadn't even *painted* the fucking painting! Then he'd begged her to put her new boots on. Obsessively, he'd gone on and on about how someone else had completed the painting while he was out getting a beer. But he took the time to admire her in the glistening boots. She had an unpleasant recollection of the day he'd pretended to read the *Tulane Drama Review* in order to show his contempt for all of them. In her pocket there had been a photostatic copy of a little-known monograph of Stekel's which he'd given her to read. She'd changed into a white crocheted dress and white sandals, then rejoined them all on the patio. First Guy, and then her father, threw pieces of incredibly charred chicken at Ralph's departing Plymouth. It seemed that everything, chicken, hot dogs, hamburgers, and ribs, was charred, and still Guy and her father talked on and on while her mother sat smiling in an Adirondack chair. Some time later, Ralph drove by again, shouting obscenities at Guy, who was praising Harold Lloyd at the expense of Chaplin and Keaton. Earlier, a letter from her Englishman, filled with amusing stories of legendary rock stars' perverted sexual practices, had repelled yet thrilled her. She often dreamed lately.

Ralph just kept driving by in his old jalopy, leaning on the horn each time he passed the house. There had been some photographs, which she loved, of a deaf, blind, and clubfooted rhythm guitarist, enclosed with his letter. Faulkner, whom Guy kept invoking in a loud voice, seemed to her distinguished, if a little seedy. She wondered if he had actually met Mick Jagger, as he claimed, at a party in London! She had tried to read

Absalom! Absalom! but returned to *Unicorn Crimson, Unicorn Grey.*
She'd hardly been surprised when Harlan removed from his sample
case a complete ensemble of ice-blue lingerie. *The Sound and the Fury*
lay on the dresser. When, flushed, she quickly pulled the panties up he
actually drooled. Although she had been as circumspect as possible
concerning the connection between her mother's stroke and the foul
letter about Mrs. Feuer and her father, Mr. Ward buried himself in his
much-read copy of *Les Constructions métalliques* for the remainder of
the evening. Ignoring what she'd said, he insisted, almost angrily, that
the color was *electric* blue. Her mother hadn't died, after all, even
though the poison-pen letter had gone into lewd detail about Mrs. Feuer
and Mr. Ward. After her mother had returned from the hospital, her
father began living in the refurbished chicken coop, saying nothing, and
existing on canned beans and chicken à la king. Her mother had been
stricken as she fussed, one cool fall evening, with the Indian corn and
autumn leaves spray on the front door. Her father denied everything,
even the fact that he knew Mrs. Feuer, and called them a gang of
Calvinist busybodies. This *couldn't* be, she thought, the reward for four
years of college! Mr. Ward, returning from what she had known for
years was his weekly rendezvous with Mrs. Feuer, almost stepped, in
the dark, on what he had first taken to be his wife's corpse. College,
then, had to be good for something. Upon her return from New Mexico,
she was surprised to find that one of the Soirée Intime's models was
April Detective, who looked, she had to admit, absolutely stunning in a
filmy peignoir. And April, as everybody knew, had never even seen the
inside of a college! The prices at the boutique were ridiculously high,
yet she still wanted, after all their troubles, to please Guy. She never
dreamed that just a few short years would find her staring in awe and
dread at *The Valley of the Shadow of Death* in Norman's living room,
while he stood behind her, his hands on her thighs. She had decided,
earlier that evening, perhaps because of something that Chet had said,
on white underclothes. Norman was something of a painter himself,
and the following morning showed her a little thing that he'd done of
Daniel Boone, dressed as a clown, in fierce struggle with what looked to
be a giant kangaroo. How she wished that she had listened to her father,
who never tired of saying that Ralph was, like all football players and
amateur painters, a repressed homosexual. In any event, from that

evening and its sordid events on, she always thought of the title of the painting as *Hell Mouth*. Norman's laughter at breakfast reminded her of Ralph's when she had complained to him about her ruined skirt. The man in the dry cleaners, as she had feared, asked her, with a lecherous grin, just what kind of a stain it was, even though he came from a closely knit community of hard-working middle-class people. Ralph had always been, she realized long after, only interested in his own selfish pleasure. Just the words, hell mouth, gave her a *frisson* of icy terror. And then Dick, whom she thought truly cared for her, began pursuing some vapid girl named Karen. She saw, with great clarity, that *he* hadn't cared that it was her best skirt either. She often dreamed lately that the mouth of Hell had opened.

She had to admit, even now, that Karen—Aileron was her surname —although not exactly pretty, had a remarkable figure. Perhaps what's-his-name's contention that Annette Lorpailleur had them all somehow in her power wasn't so farfetched after all. What galled her was that Dick had at one time, in play, liked to call her Karen! Annette somehow knew all the scandalous stories about everyone, including, to her dismay, certain incidents that had occurred in New Mexico. When she saw Harlan, still wearing the same electric-blue suit, still dragging his clubfoot along the floor, her blood almost froze. She hated Annette for being so involved with him, yet she was sickeningly attracted to her as well. When she saw her introduce Harlan and Guy to each other she thought she'd panic. And then, ten years later, there in Norm's closet were her six missing dresses and her pale blue silk tailored blouse! On the way home she refused to talk to Guy about Harlan Pungoe or about anything to do with Harlan Pungoe. It was at about this time, or so she remembered it, that Guy had first suggested that she meet an old friend of his, Norm, but she begged off. She recalled this some years later when Sheila sent her her first book of poetry, *Fretwork*, snidely inscribed "to Bunny, the belle of Boonetown." No one could ever convince her that her missing clothing didn't have something to do with Harlan's reappearance and Sheila's book. It came as a shock to her to discover that Norm had been Sheila's first lover, although in those days he had preferred to be known as Fred. On top of all these surprises, her father had begun painting miniature imitations of *Hell Mouth* on small lengths of two-by-fours. And then, of course, there was the false news that Sheila had been accidentally run over by Lou. Guy, ever more distant as his relationship with Harlan waxed, told her that he'd known her father was a fucking loony ever since the day on the patio when the other loony kept driving back and forth in his car. She didn't mention that Ralph had bought himself a used Porsche and promptly driven it into a tree. Nor did she mention that she'd secretly wanted her parents, especially her father, to hate Guy. Ralph, for some few years after being discharged from the hospital, took to coming into the city once a week to annoy her in any way he could. Guy, drinking more heavily than ever, bitterly and endlessly complained that there was never enough ice in his whiskey. Then began Ralph's letters, telling her, with relish, how *he* had been responsible for the letter that had caused her mother's stroke and her father's sojourn in the chicken coop. She blew up one hot Sunday morning and threw a mayonnaise jar full of Three Feathers into Guy's smeary, weirdly unfamiliar face. Jung, or so she thought, had written something about doubles. Contrite, she made Guy another drink, filled to the top with ice, while he sat on the fire escape weeping. All of this must have had something to do with heredity. To make matters worse, Tony Lamont called her an ignorant cunt when she ventured the opinion that his *Synthetic Ink* was Faulknerian. Psychology had a good deal to say about the causes of such vicious misogyny, something to do with mothers, to the best of her recollection. She started *Absalom! Absalom!* again. Guy had taken to ranting about Andy Warhol being the only painter of the last hundred years who mattered. She switched to *The Sound and the Fury* because of something that Lucy Taylor had said, but she couldn't remember what it was. According to Guy, Picasso was a charlatan, there was a confessional letter or something he'd read to prove it. She wanted nothing more than to go back to Long Island, as it had been, forever. Guy screamed at her that Matisse was a fucking interior decorator, then vomited on himself. On the North Shore, despite Ralph, her father's sheet-metal manuals, her mother's unmatched tableware, and their ugly Volvo, life had been easier. She had a recurrent bittersweet memory of the snow that fell on them on the beach at Provincetown. She often dreamed lately that the mouth of Hell had opened for her.

Wooden canepie

Not the usual sort of place that Lolita would sit, or for that matter, where anybody would sit, yet there she sat, perhaps in fantasy or dream, yet nonetheless she sat, shielded by its shade from the heat and glare, looking placidly on. As a rule, she'd never bothered with such attentions to herself, but she'd long since confounded the predictions that were invariably made, and many were of the opinion that they knew by whom. This was not to say, however, that the putative content of the predictions was known or even guessed at. That, in a sense however tenuous, would be too much to ask, even in the light of subsequent events.

Despite her background, her recent background, that is, Lolita didn't seem to mind, or even notice, the pedestrian, not to say gauche nature of the edifice, for such it had been termed by no less expert a personage than its architect. There had been the initial and usual grumblings about his capabilities, yet she had chosen him after all, and the product of his labors and her faith in them was now apparent for all to see. She sat then, bemused, lost in a private world of, perhaps, ambitions not yet realized. Yet there was the possibility that she was, simply and unaffectedly, rehearsing what might be termed the high points of her life. The latter were not too numerous, to be sure, so what better place for her to sit in order to call them up from a memory that had, recently, and even earlier, failed her on more occasions than she wished to be cognizant of? For example, it is rather well-established that forgotten were the dinner dance at Charmaine's, the lakeside picnic with the Carruthers brothers, the humiliating incident in the voting booth—and there were others. So her decision to locate herself beneath this rude structure, plain to the point of the primitive, may have been her attempt to shed the unnecessary, and thus reinvigorate her badly failing powers of recall.

What then if she *were* to recall the salient episodes of the life which she had so helplessly seized, which she had lived? It wasn't like Lolita to sit and simply reflect. She had always loathed nostalgia, although always may be putting it a trifle strongly. But if the congeries of past events, if congeries it was, could be separated from its usual partnership with sentiment, it cannot have been too much to cheer Lolita on in her wholehearted attempt. Many were the voices that did cheer her on, although others were predictably silent.

Well then. She sat, the cunningly ugly rude wooden structure doing the job that the architect had envisioned it being called upon to do: by Lolita, of course. No one else called upon it to do anything. Indeed, they were content to allow it just to *be*. The curious came and stared, moved on, silent or speaking in whispers, as if afraid that they would become part of Lolita's musings.

The problem for her arose almost immediately, and since it had never before been, for her, a problem, or if it had, it had been one which she had so far avoided, it struck her with overwhelming force. It was, simply, that she was unable to make any connections between or among the varied dead events that urged themselves upon her. When she entertained one event at a time, all was well. Yet when a new event rose to her mind it drove the earlier one out. Thus, when she had satisfied herself with an investigation of *this* element, she instantly had to turn her thoughts to *that* one, helplessly aware that *this* one was slipping into the oblivion whence it came, luminous. This was, and Lolita knew it, no way to survey the elements that had made up her life to its present moment. Was there any help for it? She may well have asked.

Her face, throughout what has come to be called the ordeal, never changed, but remained fixed in a beatific expression that occasionally bordered on the uncannily beautiful. It may be that Lolita triumphed, from time to time, over the violently solipsistic turmoil of her thoughts, yet who knows? On the other hand, there is some evidence that her placid visage may have expressed a surrender to utter bewilderment, that it may have been the face of a woman partially if not wholly unaware of her identity.

Her inability, at least so far, in this, her retreat, to reconstruct the entire schema of her life from the incidents which she could recall in something approaching their original clarity of outline did not, of course, preclude for her the belief that the schema did, in fact, exist. Not to put too fine a point on it, but Lolita was aware that the recalled incidents, though few, and wholly unconnected to each other in any way that she could understand, were not the whole of her past life, but that they were, surely, a proof, so-called, of its reality, if the latter is not too ingenuous a word. Her reason for sitting so quietly in what many thought a ridiculous structure, far from those she knew, and doing nothing at all, was, quite obviously, to deny, as best she could, the possibility of any *more* incidents occurring, incidents which, by the mere fact of their occurrence, would hopelessly complicate her search for the schema. In other words, she had chosen a kind of death. Some who understood this were terrified, for they realized that their own peripatetics were analogous to her stasis, but that the movements that they indulged in disguised themselves as being somehow more real than her stillness. Lolita, in short, ruthlessly demonstrated to these unfortunately perceptive few that all events are representative of death; i.e., that to look into the past is to insure the death of the present, even though that gaze is part and parcel of what might be called a story concerning long-disappeared phenomena or adventures. So much is clear.

It is somewhat embarrassing to dredge up those instances of data from the totality that was Lolita's past schema, assuming that Lolita was correct in her assumption that there was indeed a schema, since they seem so remarkably innocuous, even banal, and are made more so by the disconcerting fact that she remembered incidents only hazily, or in fragments. For instance, what was she to understand of the vast structure of her past by remembering the words *lathe operator?* Those words were revelatory, surely, of an important incident, or incidents, they were proof, so to speak, that the vast structure existed. Yet what sort of structure could be envisioned by a lost reality that asserted itself in such crabbed and opaque terms? Lolita did not know. She did know that a structure implied by these incomprehensible terms must have been made up of an infinite number of such shards, and that therefore she had existed, she had a past, her life was a highly intricate composition. *Lathe operator* was, arguably, a complement or surrogate for an infinitely variegated number of experiences which her mind would not permit her to recall. But it pleased her that *lathe operator* complemented or substituted for, or for that matter, implied, let us say, *large blue suit* or *banana split.* It was, she thought, quite possible that *large blue suit* and *banana split* were as much a part of her life's schema as was *lathe operator,* which term intruded itself so regularly and unchangingly into her thoughts. It was, perhaps, good to be ignorant of the whole structure, for then one could force it to emit whatever one wished. To see the whole and thus to prove it so is to be truly dead, whereas, as noted, Lolita was alive, though dead within her life, and contentedly so.

As she sat, turning over and over again the immutable and curious manifestations of her life, she came to realize that although none of them had any connection with any other, they did form a pattern by the fact of their *being;* yet the pattern implied only itself, and did not, in any way, bring her any nearer to a comprehension of the larger and more ordered and rational pattern from which the singular manifestations had emerged unbidden.

Lathe operator was the first of the series, in that she had had that phrase thrust upon her first. The other elements in the series, a series that repeated itself in varying combinations, were as satisfyingly impenetrable as the first. Without, then, further attempts at analysis, however unsatisfactory, of Lolita's methods, if they can be termed that, these are the elements of her past that Lolita recalled, again and again, and always with the belief that since they *were,* there must have been others, and that taken all in all they suggested, convincingly, the panorama, endlessly changing, of her past.

As *lathe operator** complemented or served as surrogate for or implied, as far as she was concerned, *large blue suit* or *banana split,* so did the importunate and repetitive element *Barnett's crucifix* complement or serve as surrogate for or imply *white shifts* or *grainy photographs; bathroom confessions, bridge deck* or *pale blue file*

---

*Lolita was astonished to realize that the diverse elements suggested by the elements from her past, which latter elements, as noted, continually recurred to her, could well have been any others; and that any or all of them in any or all combinations and permutations—ceaseless and neverending—could possess the identical relevance for and relation to the great structure of her past as did the fifty-two elements initially suggested by the twenty-six clearly recalled elements. At this point, she became convinced that her life, up to this time, had quite possibly been inextricably involved with quite possibly everything. She was, at this juncture, probably insane.

folder; orange ball, Gordon's gin or *manila envelopes; steel mistreatment, complex resolutions* or *Sazeracs; she flushing, little cabals* or *cracked window shades; stolen manuscript, broken ribs* or *pile of clothes; black basement, still twilights* or *red swans; ce soir, Spanish primer* or *Easter bonnet; slapped face, Klactoveedsedstene* or *lady's shoes; Flint, lens and shutter* or *Mus musculus; red silk, metallic fly* or *La Révocation de l'Édit de Nantes; toothpick bridge, egg cream* or *deadbeats; movie models, Ingelow's snood* or *floor plans; Conchita's sisters, black nylons* or *blue ink; hospital plunge, St. Vincent's* or *Zippo; drunken tears, quadratic equations* or *ham on rye; April showers, gross constituent unit* or *country inn; arrogant immigrant, personnage marchant vers l'horizon* or *melting snowman; mistress of metal, three-subject notebook* or *reams and reams; breaking glass, syntagma* or *amethyst crystal; false answers, mean streets* or *tape recorder; parfum intime, exotic booze* or *plot doctor; Blanche's leer, stupid writer* or *cheap blend; unknown persons, bricoleurs* or *Schiller; wooden canopy, hot sun* or *long days.*

   The final element, *wooden canopy*, asserted itself some time after the other elements which served somewhat to define Lolita's hitherto unrevealed entirety. At first, she chose to ignore it, as, indeed, she chose to ignore its congeners, *hot sun* or *long days*, for none of these seemed to have anything to do with her past. *Wooden canopy* was, of course, the element which had projected itself from the center of her present circumstances. She had chosen stasis, and its conditions, in order to preclude new experiences and thus better to isolate the past. Yet she realized, surely, that the situation which she had selected had itself, and inexorably, insisted upon its validity as an element every bit as important, or at least, as *actual*, as all the others, those recalled as well as those obliterated. Her inertia, in other words, had generated and would no doubt continue to generate elements, and their suggested elements, contributive to the overall schema of her life. There was, then, she doubtlessly admitted to herself, no *escape from life, Pungoe's adobe* or *kitchen drawer.*

Sittie of Rome

Now, because of a carefully designed plan, by means of which he is reasonably certain that you may discover various truths, or at the very least, certain insistent discrepancies among the data, however scattered, that one has been given to think of as factual, he has brought together, on a warm Sunday in Rome, a group of middle-aged women:

Sheila Henry, Joanne Lewis, Anne Kaufman, Ellen Kaufman, Antonia Harley, Conchita Kahane, Lolita Kahane, April Detective, Annette Lorpailleur, Ann Taylor Redding.

Rome?

Here, in brief, is the plan.

Seated beneath the well-known and famous pines of the old city at a large round table covered with dazzling white napery, the women will take refreshments. Brilliant white umbrella. They are pleased, it seems, to have come. Hot Roman sun, the sound of conversation and laughter, as is usual.

He is aware that their least important remarks may well be, and in all probability are, crucial to an understanding, however tenuous, of all that has been said about what you have been given to think of as their lives. One is reasonably certain of this. The sound of their conversation and laughter drifts erratically toward him.

Rome!

Women he has been given to think of as actual.

A plan: The many contradictions that you have scrupulously taken notice of may finally be resolved.

By the employment of a certain specific yet untried method one may define or at least locate those elements which may be defined or located.

By means, for instance, of a transference.

An evasion. A trick.

This, in any event, is the gist of a scheme that he will proffer you.
One is not wholly satisfied.
The women seem to be leaving. They are leaving.
Now, what.